# LEARNING CURVE

FRANKLIN U
BOOK 6

## N.R. WALKER

# COPYRIGHT

# BLURB

## COBEY GREEN

There I was, moving into the dorms at Franklin U and not into the shared party house I'd lived in my freshman year. Last year had been all about football and parties, not schoolwork. Which was why my grades tanked. Why I was one failed class away from being kicked off the team.

Why I needed to live on campus and find myself a tutor.

Funny that my new roommate just happens to *be* a tutor. Funny that he's oblivious to how hot he is. For a smart guy, he's pretty clueless. Maybe I could tutor him in how to be more outgoing in exchange for help with calculus. I could teach him how to talk to people, how to make new friends. Hell, maybe I could even help him punch his V-card.

Actually, now that I think about it . . . that's a really good idea.

## VINCENT BRANDT

And there *I* was, happy to be back at college, happy to be where I was most comfortable. Happy to be starting another school year, happy to start tutoring again so I could earn some money.

And yes, there I was, equal parts excited and dreading to see who my new roommate would be . . . until Cobey Green's smiling face appeared at the door. A huge football player loved by everyone. Gorgeous, rich, and out of the closet.

Everything I'm not.

It doesn't help that he's genuinely a nice guy. It doesn't help that I make him laugh and we can talk so easily. And it certainly doesn't help that we start having private tutoring sessions, which end up way more private than I'd ever dare imagine.

I'd ranked top of my class in every subject since the first grade, yet there I was falling stupidly in love with him.

This was going to be a hell of a year. And one very steep learning curve for both of us.

# LEARNING
## Curve

# N.R. WALKER

# ONE

## COBEY GREEN

"YOU'LL THANK US ONE DAY," Mom said.

I was in the backseat of the car, having flashbacks of when I was thirteen and my parents had enrolled me in a summer camp for mathletes instead of football. Only this time, they were moving me back to college, but not back to the fun house where I'd spent my first year. Oh no. They were moving me into the dorm. Why?

Because I was failing school.

I didn't thank them when I was thirteen, and I wasn't thanking them now.

Sure, they meant well. But come on! I was a nineteen-year-old guy on the college football team. My education was secondary to my social life. Well, and to my football life, so make that thirdary . . . if that's even a word.

And therein lay the problem. Or so my father had said. School needed to be a priority.

So yeah, a great start to the new school year.

I was trying not to be mad about it. While I wasn't thanking them, I could see their point.

Kinda.

"And who knows," Dad said brightly, eyeing me in the rearview mirror as he drove. "Your new roommate might be nice. A good influence, perhaps."

I stared.

Did I just hear him correctly?

"I'm sorry, my new room-what?"

"Your new roommate." Dad shot Mom a panicked look. "You didn't tell him?"

If Dad looked panicked, Mom looked stricken. "Didn't you?"

"Didn't tell me what?" It came out as a yell-squawk. I leaned forward through their front seats so I could try to see their faces. "A roommate?"

"All the single rooms were taken," Dad offered.

I slumped back in my seat. *They gotta be fucking kidding me.*

But no, they weren't.

"It won't hurt to make friends outside of your football buddies," Mom added. "Broaden your circle a bit. Broaden your horizons."

Cool.

*And when we get to the horizon, we can just keep on driving. Right off the fucking edge.*

"I'd rather not broaden anything, just so you know," I mumbled. "I like my football buddies just fine."

They droned on about how it won't be so bad, and it could even be great, and how it will mean more study time. Thankfully Dad realized now was not the time to lecture me again on my priorities and last year's poor grades, because all I could think about was who I was going to have to live with.

What if they were a slob? What if they left their crap all over the floor?

Oh god.

"What if they don't do laundry and our entire room stinks like a gym bag?"

Dad snorted. "You mean, like your gym bag?"

Mom turned to give me that look. You know that sorry-patronizing-grimace look that moms can do. "It's highly unlikely it could be worse than what you lived in last year, darling. And anyway, maybe your new roommate will be a quiet, clean, and considerate person." Then she mumbled under her breath, "Unlike whom you lived with last year."

"The guys I lived with last year were just fine," I grumbled. "They're my friends. My teammates. And what if this roommate person is super weird? Like crazy-weird."

"I'm sure they'll be fine," Dad said. "And if they're not, if you really can't live with them, then you can see about changing rooms. Just give it a couple of weeks. Who knows . . ." He gave me a hopeful glance in the rearview mirror. "They could turn out to be someone great."

I sighed.

Now, I was normally an optimistic guy, always trying to look on the bright side. But this semester was going to blow.

## VINCENT BRANDT

My new roommate was Cobey Green.

Cobey freaking Green.

He, of course, had no idea who I was. Which probably wasn't surprising, let's be real. Everyone at Franklin U knew who Cobey Green was. He was the incredibly popular, six-foot-three linebacker for the Kings, totally gorgeous, with a killer trademark grin. If that hadn't been enough to annoy my cynical little heart, I'd never heard anyone say a bad word about him.

"Hey, man," he'd said, carrying a box in. I'd opened the door, saw him holding said box with the aforementioned killer grin, and I'd stood there like an idiot. "Name's Cobey. Your new roomie."

It took a second for my brain to function. "Oh, sure." I stood aside. "Come in. I, uh . . . I moved in already and put my stuff on the left."

Cobey put the box on his bed. "I'm cool with whatever," he said, still wearing that ridiculously stunning grin. "Oh, this is my mom and dad. Sorry, I didn't catch your name."

"I'm Vincent Brandt."

There was a forty-year-old dad version of Cobey, clearly where he got his height from. And a woman, from whom he'd very obviously inherited his smile.

"Hi, Vincent," his mom said. She had a huge bag of bedding. "I'm Sheree, and this is Chris."

I gave Cobey's parents a smile and a nod. "Nice to meet you."

The room was small enough as it was—with two single beds, two desks, two closets—but now with three tall people all looking at me, it was kinda crowded. And I was never good with parents.

"I'll, uh, I'll let you get settled in," I said, shoving my hands in my jean's pockets.

"Oh, we didn't mean to make you uncomfortable," Sheree said. "You can stay. This is your room."

"No, it's fine. It's not that." I gave them my best smile and pointed to the door. "I have to go see about a . . . tutor program thing. In the tutoring center . . . it's in the library."

"Oh, a tutor program." Chris's eyes lit up and he gave Cobey an excited nod. "See, son? Vincent here's in the tutor program too. There's no shame in needing a tutor."

Cobey was clearly horrified, and he hissed, "Dad!"

Oh god.

That was my cue to leave.

"Nice to meet you," I said again, edging my way around them toward the door. "Oh, Cobey, you might not want to open the blind. It fell down before."

He gave me an apologetic smile, and after giving him a nod, I bailed. I did have to go to the library to see about the tutor program; that wasn't a lie. And the room was too small for four people anyway. Giving them the space to get settled and organized without me sitting on my bed like an awkward lump, getting even more awkward questions from Cobey's parents . . .

No thanks.

Not today.

In the tutoring center, I found Rafe behind an armful of books. "Hey, Vincent," he said warmly. "Glad to see you back, man."

Rafael was a junior English major, and we'd been friends since my first day there. I didn't have many friends. Like maybe three I could name. We didn't hang out often, or at all, really, but we were friends enough to strike up a conversation. Like now.

I took half his burden of books. "Hey. Yeah, it's good to be back. How was your summer?"

"Not bad. Time with the fam, and earned some money helping my dad. How about you?"

"Yeah, much the same," I lied, on both counts, and quickly changed the subject. "Just met my new roommate."

"Oh? Who is it?"

"Cobey Green."

Rafe put the books down and gave me a smile. "Oh, he's a nice guy."

That was the consensus. Absolutely everyone at Franklin U knew him and liked him. I wasn't sure why that annoyed me.

Jealousy?

No.

I just didn't hold people who coasted in high regard. The type of people who had everything come easy: money, social life, sports. And Cobey was the epitome of that. Superstar football player, tall, gorgeous, rich, friends with everyone, had loving parents.

He was also out and proud.

He was literally every single thing I wished I was . . . but wasn't.

Was that his fault? No. Was any of his good fortune his fault? Also no.

Was I being an ass with my generalizing, broad-sweeping, stereotypical assumptions?

Possibly yes.

"Yeah, I'm sure he's great," I added. "He's gotta be better than the guy I roomed with last year."

Rafe chuckled. "We can only hope." I helped him sort through the books in a comfortable silence for a while. "Please tell me you're here to sign up for the tutor program?"

"Oh, yeah. That's what I came in here for."

"You mean you didn't come in just to see me?"

I rolled my eyes, but he did make me smile. "Oh, sure. That too."

See? I sucked at the whole friend thing.

"We're having a bit of a welcome back party this weekend." Rafe handed me the clipboard. "You should come."

I took the clipboard, my introverted heart panicking at the mention of a social outing. "Oh."

He laughed. "The look on your face . . ."

"No, I could come," I tried, regretting it as soon as I'd said it. "Who else will be there?"

He looked at me, obviously deciding not to laugh when he realized I was trying to be serious. "Just the usual crew. It's just a small thing. You know how we are."

I nodded. I did know. They were good people. My kind of people: quiet and studious.

I filled out the tutoring information, and we chatted a while. I liked Rafe. He was chill and nothing fazed him much.

But I couldn't put off going back to my room forever.

Cobey was alone in our room when I got back. "Oh, hey," I said. "Your folks gone already?"

"Yeah, they had to go back home," he replied and nodded to the window. "Dad fixed the blinds."

I sat on my bed, trying not to let things get awkward. "So is, uh, is home far?"

Great job, Vincent. Don't make it awkward by asking a straight-up personal question.

"Nah," he said effortlessly. "San Diego. What about you?"

"San Luco."

"Ah, sweet. This is your hometown."

Not far enough for me.

"My parents just wanted to make sure I moved in okay," he added. "I was in Mundell last year and my grades tanked." He sighed. "It's a catch-22. My grades were shit because of football. You know, games, training, the social side of it. It takes up so much of my time and studying isn't a real priority for me. But if I don't maintain at least a 2.0 GPA, I can't play football. It's part of my scholarship deal. I just scraped through. Coach was pissed, but my parents went kinda nuclear. And here I am. In the dorm."

Plenty of guys maintained a football and school ratio, and they managed just fine. I didn't doubt it wasn't a difficult seesaw of commitment, but I had to wonder if there was more to Cobey's story.

"It's not so bad here in the dorm," I said. "Not as much fun as the Mundell house, I bet. But that's probably the point."

"That's exactly the point. Apparently." His grin was something special, and it was easy to see why people liked him.

He'd put up some posters and pictures on his side of the room above his bed. There was a vintage Coca-Cola poster that was kinda cool, and there were some group photos, team photos, all smiling faces. There was a poster of Post Malone wearing a dress and a poster of Jesus . . . no, Mary . . . no, wait. "Is that Adam Driver?"

Cobey burst out laughing. "Yep. It's funny as fuck." Then he stopped, his eyes quickly finding mine. "Uh, if you don't like it, I can take it down. I didn't mean to offend you, or anyone. Shit. Sorry."

I snorted. "No. I'm not offended. It *is* kinda funny." Then I nodded to a small rectangular flag stuck with the photos. "Is that the bi flag?"

His gaze shot to mine. "Do you have a problem with that?"

"Oh, no. Absolutely not," I replied quickly, trying not to panic. The last thing I needed was for him not to like me just two minutes into the year. "No problem. Actually, I kinda like it. That you . . ."

*Shut up, Vincent.*

*Just shut up.*

"That I'm what?"

Gawd.

I wanted to die. I certainly didn't want to answer, but his stare was drilling into me. It made my mouth dry. "That you're, you know, out and proud."

"Oh." He was clearly relieved, but then I could almost hear the penny drop. He stared. "Oh."

Panic struck me. "No, it's not like that," I said. Except it was. "I'm not . . . I'm not . . ."

He tilted his head. Patient. Curious. "You're not what?"

"Out," I blurted. "I'm not out."

Way to go, Vincent. Announce that to a complete stranger. Something you've never told anyone, and you just blurt it out to Cobey freaking Green. Of all the people. One of the most popular sophomore guys at college.

Way to fucking go.

## COBEY

"It's cool," I said. "I won't tell anyone."

Vincent looked like he'd swallowed something sharp and sour. "I, uh . . . I, god, I have no idea why I just said that. To you. Out loud."

I gave him a smile my grandma would call cheeky. "I've got a likable face. People tell me random stuff all the time."

He still really looked uncomfortable. Panicked, even. I wanted him to know he could talk to me about this stuff. Being a popular out-and-proud queer guy in college came with responsibility. "So," I hedged. "Are you gay, bi, trans, pan, ace?"

This question surprised him. "Oh. I'm, um, gay."

"Got a boyfriend?" I wiggled my eyebrows. "Someone who'll be paying little visits to our room? We can establish a code if you want. Like a towel on the door or something?"

He scoffed, and his cheeks turned pink. "No. No boyfriend." He cleared his throat. "I've, um . . . I've never had a boyf . . ." His words trailed off, his cheeks now a heated red. "I don't know why I keep just telling you this shit. Out loud. To your face."

I laughed and pointed to my face. "It's my face, I swear. People just blurt stuff out all the time."

His smile softened, and I think he appreciated my effort to make him feel comfortable. He wiped his palms on his thighs. "What about you?" he asked. "Boyfriend? Girlfriend?"

"Nope. Neither." He seemed surprised by this as well. "Is that so hard to believe?" I asked with a grin.

He made a face. "No, I just thought . . . I just thought you'd have a long line of people you'd have to fight off with a stick."

That made me laugh. "Well, the line is long, but I don't fight them off."

It took him a second to catch on to what I meant. I knew the second he'd realized because his cheeks blushed a deeper red. "Oh, right. Yeah, of course."

I shrugged. "What's not to like about sex, right?"

I thought he blushed red before, but no. *This* was red. A deep scarlet bloomed up his cheeks and down his neck. I was a little taken aback how much I liked that.

Vincent was a very good-looking guy. Very nerdy. Floppy dark hair, pale skin, glasses, blue-gray eyes, pink lips, and a fucking blush.

Damn.

"Yeah, yeah, of course," he replied, then pulled an old laptop from his backpack, and sitting against his headboard, he flipped it open. "Have you logged in to see your syllabi yet?"

And just like that, he changed the subject. Clearly he wasn't too comfortable talking about sex. Maybe talking about personal things five minutes into our first conversation was too much for him. I had no issue talking about whatever, but he obviously did. And that was okay.

"Nah, not yet." I side-eyed my laptop. "My very strategic plan of attack was to put off the inevitable for as long as possible."

Vincent smiled. "Sound plan."

# TWO

## VINCENT

THE NEXT FOUR days went fast. School started, so that kept me busy enough, in conjunction with my new tutoring schedule—which included one mix-up, two new additions, and one cancellation already—all while trying to avoid my new roommate.

Yes, avoid.

Why?

Because Cobey goddamn Green was gorgeous. He was cute. He would smile a certain way that sent my stomach into a jittery nosedive. He had one dimple that short-circuited my brain. He talked in a way that was both slow and sweet.

And twice now, two-freaking-times out of a possible four days, he'd come into our room after a run, his gym shirt clinging to him like a second skin. And from this I have learned three things about myself.

The first thing was the scent of his deodorant and sweat made me lightheaded. Honestly, who knew it was an aphrodisiac?

The second thing was that I'd never once thought of jocks as attractive. The ego that usually accompanied a muscular physique was normally a turn off for me. The jock boys-club, that I have never been part of, normally sent me running in the opposite direction.

But he was different.

The third thing, and possibly the most important, was that Cobey held full eye contact when we talked. And I had no clue, no clue whatsoever, just how much I valued that.

It was intense, the way his gaze locked on like a laser. And he listened, like actually really listened. His blue eyes saw right into me, hypnotized me.

And I could see why everyone liked him. Before I'd actually met him, I just assumed everyone adored him because he was the gorgeous jock football player, Mr. Popular, great-at-everything kind of guy.

But it was more than that and I could see that now. Everyone liked him because he treated them with respect and kindness. When he asked how your day was, he listened to your reply. He was just a genuinely decent guy.

And did I mention gorgeous?

I hated that he was so good-looking.

It made holding a conversation with him so much harder. Or maybe it was the eye contact itself.

It was probably the eye contact.

It was definitely the eye contact.

Something else I learned about myself and the wizardry of his eye contact was that I'd lose all brain functionality and blurt stupid shit out to him. Highly personal and very private secret stuff. Like coming out to him. Because what the actual hell?

And having him talk about sex?

Heaven help me.

It was the most exciting and thrilling and horrifying thing to ever happen to me. Just talking about sex with him . . . Thankfully I could stop my malfunctioning brain before I blurted out that, no, I couldn't contribute to the sex conversation because I'd never had sex before.

Not even remotely close.

Like I could ever tell Cobey Green *that*.

"Hey." Rafe greeted me as I walked into the library. He put his pencil down. "How's your day been?"

"Same old. How about you?"

"Same old." He pushed the clipboard he was working on to the side. "Always late adjustments, you know how it is."

I nodded. There were always amendments as students settled into the new school year: classes were changed, schedules were fine-tuned, and reality settled in. "Let me know if you need me to take on any more."

He winced. "You're already full, man. Take on any more and it'll start affecting your grades. It's why they cap it."

"I could always use the money." Because that was the truth.

His face softened. "I know, and I'm sorry. But they have limits for a reason. Tutoring everyone else will do you no favors if you start failing your own classes."

I raised an eyebrow and he laughed. "I mean it," he added. "Yeah, it's all easy to you now, Mr. Genius, but it won't always be. You need a life outside of schoolwork too. Or even time to sleep. I hear that's good for you."

I was about to reply that he could use some of his own medicine when a girl walked in, clutching her laptop satchel, looking kinda lost.

"Can I help you?" Rafe asked, all kind smiles.

"I have a tutorial with a Mr. Vincent Brandt?" she said, like it was a question.

Rafe gestured to me. "The one and only."

She looked at me, giving me a quick up and down, very clearly surprised that I was a tutor. Her tutor, no less. I was used to this reaction. People usually took one look at my old, cheap, no-name jeans and shirt, at my old Converse high-tops, and they couldn't reconcile that image with my IQ.

As if only the smart people were super rich.

Same old.

"Hi," I said, giving her a bright smile. "Tessa, is it?"

She finally smiled back. Out of relief, I think. "Yes!" She shook my offered hand. "Nice to meet you."

We sat at a table and she took out her laptop, and we spent most of our first session going over expectations, syllabi, and deadlines. Tessa was a junior, and if she was bothered by me being only a sophomore, just a few minutes into our session, she was over it. She was actually really sweet and just needed some help with statistics.

Advanced stats were no problem for me. And much to the horror of most of the people I tutored, I actually enjoyed it.

When our session was done and we were packing up, I heard a familiar voice talking to Rafe.

Cobey.

Fresh from football practice, by the looks of him—his gear bag at his feet, wearing gym shorts and a sleeveless shirt with darkened sweat patches, his hair damp.

God help me.

I couldn't hear exactly what Rafe said, but they both looked around the tutoring center at all the full desks, and when Cobey saw me, he did a double take.

Tessa packed up her laptop, smiling and happier now she was on the right path. We said goodbye, confirming our session for next week, and I walked her as far as Rafe's desk.

"See you next week," I said, waving her off. I gave Cobey a smile. "Hey."

"Oh, hey," he replied.

"Whatcha doing?"

Rafe answered. "He was looking to register for the tutor program. I was just telling him how the schedule is full, but people do drop out so it's not all bad news."

Cobey made a face. "I was supposed to do it the other day."

"Oh," I began, but Rafe was quick to interrupt.

"I told him all the tutor's schedules were full."

"It's okay," Cobey said. "It's my fault. I got busy with football and, you know, avoiding anything school related."

I was smiling at him because why did he have to be so damn cute?

And sweaty and so damn sexy?

For god's sake.

"I just left weight training," he volunteered. "And the days I could do any tutoring would be kinda limited because of football, practice and games and shit. I uh, I didn't realize when you said you had to register for the tutor program that you meant you were the tutor." He ran his hand through his hair. "So that's kind of embarrassing."

Oh shit.

"No it's not," I said quickly. "It's not embarrassing at all to want to improve. It's admirable."

He picked up his gym bag and turned to Rafe. "I guess I should put my name on the waiting list then."

"Sure thing," Rafe said. "Calculus, right?"

"Ah, yeah," Cobey replied.

Rafe's gaze cut to mine because, of course those would be my specialties, but his eyes told me not to say anything. My schedule was full, yes. But come on . . .

More students left and more came in and a guy came up to the desk, recognizing Cobey immediately. "Hey, man," he said, grinning. They did some weird hand-bump thing.

"Hey, Bumbles," Cobey said.

Bumbles?

"Ready for the game this weekend?"

Ah. A football friend. I should have guessed.

"As I'll ever be."

"You were on fire the other day." Bumbles looked at me and Rafe then, seemingly remembering where he was. Or that he needed to explain what he was doing here. "Oh, I have a six o'clock session with Vincent. For economics."

Rafe and Cobey both looked at me. I waved my hand like an idiot. "Hi, Brett."

"Back for another year," he said with a shrug. Then he clapped

Cobey on the shoulder. "Gotta try to get this math shit to sink in. Later, man."

"Yeah, later." Cobey gave a nod, smiled at Rafe, then looked at me. "See ya later."

He was either confused or baffled, I wasn't sure.

"Yeah, see you later," I said, then Brett and I went back to my table.

The fact I'd tutored Brett last year as well made his nickname a surprise. "Bumbles?"

Brett laughed. "Coach had the player list when I was a freshman and he just had my first initial instead of my name. He called me Bee for half the first season, then the boys called me Bumble Bee, and it stuck. You didn't know people call me that?"

I shook my head. *How would I know that?* "No."

He sighed. "You wound my ego, man."

I probably should've known that, given he was another super popular guy on the football team. But like I said before, I didn't have much time for jocks or sports.

But I had time for Brett, the senior business student who needed my help keeping his grades up.

I chuckled. "I've been told I need to get out of the classroom a bit more."

He laughed, not outwardly agreeing but not disagreeing either.

We got through our session easily enough, but I kept thinking about Cobey. He needed a tutor in subjects that were my specialty. I wanted to help him, even though my schedule was full. But could I tutor my roommate? Or would it be weird?

Probably too weird.

## COBEY

I was screwed.

Unless I could get into the tutor program, my parents were going to be pissed at me. And it was my fault. Dad told me to do it on my first day. Everyone told me to do it on move-in day. But did I?

Nope.

I got busy.

Busy with training and pregame stuff, but also with seeing the guys. We had some catching up to do! I hadn't seen them over the break and I'd missed hanging out.

I also had to navigate a new roommate, who was quiet and a bit nerdy, if I was being honest. And totally fucking hot in his own way. He'd lie on his bed to read his books, leaning against the headboard, wearing old gray sweatpants and a T-shirt.

He'd read and make notes, chewing on his bottom lip every so often, not even meaning to be sexy as hell. And I'd pretend not to .stare at him like a fucking creep.

I wanted to crawl up his body, toss the book away, take his glasses off, and have my way with him.

Which was why I went running every night.

I'd swing past my old house or Shenanigans, the college bar, just to see the guys. To hang out.

But mostly to avoid wanting to rail my roommate.

The nerdy types were not usually my kind of thing, but fucking hell, there was something about him. Something quiet and confident that really turned me on. Like he knew he was smart but didn't boast about it. He knew he was good-looking but didn't play on it. He was a freaking tutor, for god's sake. A sophomore tutoring seniors. Like, what the actual fuck? Obviously he was super smart, but he wasn't arrogant or a dick about anything, and there was something really refreshing about that. I spent most of my time around guys who boasted about every single thing, and to have Vincent be the opposite of that was kinda great.

And god, I really wanted to rail him.

Which is why I was running *again*, and why I found myself at Shenanigans on my way home. Anything to distract myself.

Shenanigans was always jumping. Good food, great atmosphere, loud and crowded, and they let underagers like me in. Not to drink alcohol, of course. Which would be impossible for me, considering almost every person in San Luco knew me as a hot shot linebacker, making a name for himself at just nineteen. It made trying to pass as a twenty-one-year-old impossible.

"Hey," a familiar voice said, followed by a warm hand on my shoulder.

I turned to see Bumbles.

Great. Just great.

Because that meant he was about to talk about the very someone I was trying not to think about.

"So, you rooming with Vincent? That's funny."

And there it was. *Vincent*. I wasn't entirely sure what was funny about it, but whatever. Maybe that the smartest and the not-smartest were sharing a room.

"Ah, yeah. Just new this year. Been a few days so far. He seems okay."

"He is," Bumbles replied. "Not gonna lie, when I first met him last year and he was supposed to tutor me, I was like no fucking way. He was a freshman and I was a junior. How could he tutor me?" He shook his head. "But the guy's a genius."

A genius.

Great.

"Yeah. He reads a lot," I replied lamely.

Bumbles raised his beer and took a sip. "I just finished my session with him. Thought I'd have a brewski before heading home."

"Yeah, I was late getting registered for the tutor program," I admitted. "My own fault. Got busy. You know how it is."

He nodded sympathetically. "Yeah, it fills up pretty quick, but people do drop out, so you might be okay. But hey, with Vincent being your roommate and all, you might get some personal lessons."

He seemed to be implying something about that, but I ignored it.

Brax was working the bar, like he was most nights. He tapped the counter. "Hey, Cobey. Can I get you anything?"

"Just a water'd be great. Thanks."

He filled a glass and put it in front of me. "You been in a few nights this week already. Running again?"

"Yeah. Trying to get my fitness up. Thought I'd see if any of the guys were in."

"Nah. Not your boys. It's the swim team tonight. And lacrosse." His boyfriend was on the lacrosse team, so his smile needed no explanation.

"Yeah, yeah," Bumbles said. "Just cause you're getting it on the regular doesn't mean you need to rub it in."

Brax laughed and went off to serve other customers, but the conversation circling around to sex was doing me no favors. I downed the water, clapped Bumbles on the shoulder, and bid him goodnight.

I walked back to the dorm.

Maybe Vincent wouldn't be there when I got back . . .

Which was stupid. He was allowed to be in our room. And me avoiding him wasn't right, either. I didn't want him to think I didn't like him. Because I did! I mean, I barely knew him, but still . . .

I needed to come up with a new plan. I needed to play offense instead of defense.

I needed to stop being such a wuss. What the hell was I so afraid of? That he'd turn me down? Or that he'd say yes?

*Get your head in the game, Cobey.*

What did Coach say about training? Do group exercises and drills until your individual program was nailed down.

Being tutored was just like an individual program, right? And if I couldn't do that, then I'd just do the group drills in the mean-time. I'd follow their lead, do as they did.

That could work, right?

Vincent studied and read books every night in our room. Usually while I listened to music or scrolled my socials. So if I did what he did, then it had to be the next best thing.

Right?

*Okay, so that's my plan.*

"Oh, hey," I said, acting surprised to see him. He was at his desk, several books open in front of him.

"Hey," he said. He looked me up and down. "Does practice ever stop?"

I looked down at my gym clothes. "Nah, I was just out running again."

"For fun?"

I flopped down on my bed, grinning. "Yep." I pulled my bag over and took out my laptop, ready to put my new plan into action.

"Hey, uh," he said, "so I tried to tell Rafe I could take on one more in the tutor program, but he said no."

"Oh, that's okay, no problem," I replied. "Thanks anyway. I guess if someone drops out, then I'm on the list."

He took his glasses off. "Yeah. Um, I'll let you know if I hear anything."

My brain was stuck trying to decide if he was sexier with the glasses, without the glasses, or while he was taking them off.

*Get your head in the game, Cobey.*

Yeah right.

I nodded to his books. "Whatcha reading?"

He groaned out a sigh. "Oh, this is partial differential equations," he shrugged. "Thought I better check I was on the right track for one of my premed sessions."

He tutored premed students.

Right.

"You're reading that for fun?"

He almost smiled. "I'd rather do this than jogging for fun."

I laughed. "Touché."

Except that most able-bodied people could run to some degree. Few people could do specialized math, but okay.

"How do you know stuff that's so advanced?" I asked. I nudged my calculus textbook. "I suck at shit for my own class."

"Oh, well . . ." He looked at the books in front of him, then back to me. "How are you so good at football?"

I wasn't expecting that. "I dunno. I've always been good at it. Been playing since I was real little. And a lot of practice and training."

He tapped his pen on the open textbook. "Same. Football comes natural to you. This comes natural to me."

I'd not really ever thought of that before. "Hm. I guess."

Speaking of which . . . *Remember your plan, Cobey.*

With a sigh, I pulled my textbook closer and started reading.

# THREE

## VINCENT

COBEY SAT on his bed and started reading his calculus book. For about five minutes. Then he scooted up the bed to lean against the headboard and read some more. For another three minutes.

Then he sighed.

Then he kicked his running shoes off, scowled at his book, and read for another two minutes.

Then he took his laptop and clicked away on the keys for a bit but mostly stared at the screen. I thought he might be reading, but after a while I realized he was staring into space.

Not just staring. He was frowning.

God. *Should I say something? I should say something, but what?* Why was being around people so hard?

*Do it, Vincent. Say something . . .*

"Are you okay?" I asked.

He slid his laptop off his lap and shot up off the bed. "Yep. Gonna take a shower. Maybe get something to eat. Can't concentrate."

He grabbed his toiletry kit and a handful of clothes and was gone.

Okay then.

He most definitely was not okay.

He came back about fifteen minutes later wearing sweatpants and a football T-shirt, his hair damp, smelling of soap and deodorant. I wasn't even mad that the smell of his sweat was gone, because a freshly showered Cobey was just as hot.

He threw his toiletry kit onto his desk and ran his hand through his hair. "I need to eat," he said. Was he nervous? He seemed nervous. "Did you want to come? Just down to the dining hall. Nothing fancy. It's totally cool if you don't want to, I just thought I'd ask because it's kind of late and you've been busy with the tutor program, and whatever. Have you eaten? I probably should've asked that first. Or did you want to keep studying?"

"Do you want me to go to dinner with you?" I asked, unable to hide my surprise.

"Not *dinner* dinner, like a date or nothing. I didn't mean it like that. I just thought I'd ask." His cheeks were red, and he headed for the door. "It's okay, no big deal."

"Wait," I said quickly, and he thankfully stopped. I didn't entirely mean to say it out loud, but now I had to follow up with more. At least I thought that's how conversations went. "Sure, I could eat. I usually miss dinner because of my schedules and stuff. But food sounds good." I pulled on my shoes, trying not to overthink why he was asking me to dinner and also trying not to freak out because Cobey freaking Green just asked me to dinner. Even though he'd been pretty clear on the fact it was not a date, but still . . . "I'm not used to people asking me to join them," I admitted. Then I made a face because that was not exactly true. "Or I'm not used to agreeing when people ask me."

He held the door for me and we walked down the corridor. "Why don't you agree when people ask you to join them?"

"I'm busy a lot." I winced. "And the most obvious reason is that I'm not very good with people."

Cobey clearly didn't have that problem. We passed two girls near the end of the corridor. "Hi, Cobey," they both said.

"Hey," he replied.

Next it was a guy carrying a laundry hamper. "Hey, Green. Good luck this weekend!"

"Thanks, man."

Then it was a couple in the vestibule. Cobey held the door for them. "Thanks, Cobey!"

"No problem," he replied.

Then people in the dining hall. "Hey, Cobey," a guy said. Then a girl. Then two girls. And he never stopped smiling. He was always polite, gracious.

By the time we grabbed our trays and sat at a table, I felt very scrutinized. "Is it like this everywhere you go?" I asked.

"Like what?"

Christ. *This was his normal?*

"Every single person knows you," I said. "Likes you. Speaks to you. Smiles at you."

"I'm a very likable guy," he replied with a grin.

"Clearly." I stabbed some salad with my fork. "I think people are wondering who I am and what the hell I'm doing with you. They're staring."

He looked around then. "Who's staring?"

He was so oblivious, so used to every single person knowing who he was.

"I don't see anyone staring." He frowned as he chewed a mouthful of food, scanning the dining hall, none too covertly.

"So maybe people aren't *staring*," I allowed. "But there are definitely some glances, some side-eyes. Pretty sure that table near the door are trying to figure out who I am and what I'm doing with you. Or," I said, "they know who I am, and they are completely perplexed as to what I'm doing with you. Maybe they're making up wild scenarios or taking bets."

His eyes cut to mine, concerned. "Taking bets?"

"Yeah. Like a wager. Five bucks they think we have to do some group project because there's no way you'd be seen in public with me."

Cobey frowned, the fork in his hand forgotten. "I don't know what's worse. That you're judging them, assuming them to be assholes, or that you honestly think so little of yourself. Why wouldn't I be seen in public with you?"

I felt genuinely rebuked.

"Sorry. I'm not assuming they're assholes." I shrugged. I kinda was. "Not them in particular, but people in general tend to be . . . assholes. Sorry if they're friends of yours."

"They're not. Not really. I mean, I'm friends with a lot of people."

"I've realized." I stabbed my mac and cheese. "And it's not that I necessarily think little of myself. I'm just aware of what people think."

"For real?" He smirked. "You can tell what people think? What am I thinking right now?"

He was joking, clearly. I might have rolled my eyes. "You're wishing you ordered pizza from anywhere but here instead of that salad."

He grinned. "Wow. You actually can read my mind." He pushed his empty plate away. "It's not so bad. I gotta watch what I eat. I had a huge lunch of carbs and protein, so it evens out."

God, his entire life was diet, exercise, training. Football, football, football. He was dedicated, that was for sure.

I offered him my hardly touched plate of mac and cheese. "Want this? I won't tell your coach if you don't. You're a huge guy. You need to eat more than salad. Plus, you went jogging again today. Consider it a reward."

He eyed the pasta. He definitely wanted it, so I pushed it closer to him. He took one mouthful and his excitement ended as soon as the taste registered. Or maybe it was the texture.

He struggled to swallow it and quickly washed it down with his glass of water. "Have mercy, that's awful."

I snorted. "It's not that bad." I mean, college food wasn't good either, but it sure as hell beat no food.

He shook his head and pushed the offending plate away from both of us. "On a scale of one to fucking awful, it's an eleven. You said it was a reward. That is not a reward. That's not even a punishment. It's a crime."

I laughed and looked over to the service area. "Want me to get you something else?"

Smiling, he shook his head. "No, but thank you." He was quiet for a bit, but he kept his eyes on me. "So, what's your major?"

"I'm double majoring in math and tech science."

He stared. "So you *are* a genius. Bumbles wasn't joking."

"Bumbles? He mentioned me?"

"Ah, yeah, I ran into him earlier. After your tutor session. He said you were a nice guy and a genius. I didn't realize he meant literally. But I guess if you are tutoring seniors . . ."

"Oh." I wasn't sure why I was embarrassed. "Uh. I haven't done an actual IQ test since high school, so the results could be outdated."

"But? Was it high?"

I smiled. "It was okay."

He nodded. "So it was high. Higher than Snoop Dog and Willie Nelson locked in a dispensary?"

I laughed. "Maybe not that high."

"So what do those degrees get you?"

"Data scientist. It's just a fancy term for data analyst." Kind of.

"Oh. I assumed you were going to say designing rockets at NASA or some shit."

I found myself smiling at him. I don't know why I found him so easy to talk to. "Well, I could. But honestly, there isn't any money in academia or math science. I love math science, actually. But data science is where the money is. Those tech-giants pay big dollars for someone who can understand it. Especially predictive analytics."

"So, why Franklin University? I thought all real geniuses went to somewhere like MIT or Harvard."

"Because FU is the only one that offered a full scholarship." *And I had no way to get to the east coast . . .*

This surprised him. "Oh, well that's cool. Hell yeah, that makes sense to come here then."

"What about you? What's your major?"

His lip pulled down in one corner and he sighed. "Business. But I'm just here for football. Coach says there's a good chance I could go pro. If I don't fail, that is. School was never my strong suit. God, put me on the football field before a classroom any day."

"Having a business degree would be helpful for you though. I'd imagine pro football players need to know how to manage their finances and endorsements. Or whatever it is football players have."

He smiled. "Well, if I make the big time, I'm paying someone to do all that shit for me." He studied me for a second. "You really don't know football, do you?"

I shook my head. "Not at all."

"You watched some of our games last year though, right?"

I grimaced. "Uh, no. Sorry."

Just then, three people walked past. Two girls, one guy. "Hey, Cobey! Good luck on Saturday."

He gave them his killer smile. "Thanks."

"What's on Saturday?" I asked.

"Football."

"Oh."

"You should come. It's a home game. I can't believe you've never watched the Kings play."

I made a face. "I've never actually watched any football before. Of any team. Not even on TV."

He stared at me as though I'd spoken in tongues, a language so bizarre and foreign, he was momentarily stunned. "Never?"

I shrugged. "Never."

"Then that settles that. You have to come on Saturday. As my roommate, you're obligated. It's a rule."

"A rule?"

"I'm sure it's in the FU code of conduct."

"I'm sure it's not."

"Did you have plans for Saturday?"

"Well," I hesitated. "I was invited to a thing with Rafe, but I wasn't actually going to go."

"Rafe? The tutor guy? Is he your . . . are you . . . ?"

It took me a second. He thought Rafe and I were dating. "Oh no. God no, not like that. He's just a friend."

"Why weren't you going to go? If he invited you?"

"It's what we do. He invites me to stuff, and I don't go." I cringed at how that sounded. "I'm not very good with people. Or in crowds, or parties, or even just with one person."

"You're doing all right with me."

"Because you're easy to talk to. We've already established that. And I can honestly say I think I've said more words to you today than I have any other person all week."

"So you just go to class, tutor people, and study. That's it?"

I nodded. "Yeah. I also sleep, eat, and participate in personal hygiene rituals."

He laughed. "Personal hygiene is important. As someone who trains and practices in tight Lycra, with a lot of other guys, I can tell you, yes, it is very important."

I scrunched my nose up. "Gross. But parties aren't my thing. I tend to avoid group social outings."

"But you'll come to the game on Saturday."

"Uh . . ." That was *the* definition of a group social outing. I could only presume on a very large scale.

"Excellent."

"That wasn't a yes."

"It's in the roommate rule book." Then he leaned in. "If you tell me you honestly struggle with large crowds, I'll drop it. But if it's just because you hate people in general, then the rule stands."

I scowled at him. "I don't hate all people."

"Just the ones you have to deal with."

"Some of them, yes."

"Then that settles it. You're coming on Saturday. I'll get you a pass, so there'll be no excuses."

Goddammit.

His grin was a victorious one. The kind he probably wore when they won all their football games.

I'd never had anyone coerce me into a social outing before. Or basically force me to go, even getting me a ticket. I shouldn't have liked it now. But Cobey was so cute, in a huge jock-football-player kind of way. And he was genuinely a really good guy as well. I liked that he was oblivious to his own popularity.

People in the dining hall still turned to see us. They mostly looked at him, fondly too, like he was some popularity god. Yet he didn't even notice. He spoke to me, held eye contact with me, laughed with me, like we were the only two in the room.

No one had ever made me feel that special.

"Okay, I'll go," I relented, trying not to smile.

His grin widened. "Awesome."

I should have added a caveat. "As long as I don't have to talk to anyone."

His smile faltered. "Not even me?"

"You'll be busy doing your footballing. I'll be in the back row of the audience trying to understand what's going on."

He laughed. "Footballing. Audience. You crack me up."

I wasn't sure what was so funny, but okay. It looked like I was going to the game . . . at his invitation. Not that it meant anything. Cobey was literally the nicest guy to every single person he ever met. He probably invited a dozen people to every game.

*Don't think you're anything special, Vincent.*

I smiled despite the voice in my head. "Well, I suppose I should get back to the books."

He groaned. "Yeah. Same. I guess."

So we went back to our room, back to our studies—me at my

desk and Cobey on his bed. The single bed looked tiny with his huge body on it. And it didn't take more than ten minutes before he was back to fidgeting.

He went from lying down on his back to sitting up, to leaning against the headboard, to lying down on his stomach, back to sitting up. He'd turn a page, squint at it for a while, then turn another.

It was the same calculus book he'd been reading earlier, and it was pretty clear to me that he wasn't getting anything done.

"Not feeling it?" I asked, nodding to the textbook.

He tossed it toward his backpack. "Nope. Nothing's going in today."

"How do you normally study?"

He scrubbed his hands over his face. "I don't."

Oh.

He flopped back down onto his back with a sigh. "Might just listen to some tunes. Didn't mean to interrupt you."

"You didn't interrupt me." I gently closed my textbook. I was pretty sure I had a good handle on the subject. I felt bad for Cobey though. I didn't like to see him struggle. I didn't like to see anyone struggle, but him especially.

It also didn't help that he was lying down, wearing sweat shorts and a shirt that rode up a little. I could see the beginning of some very flat abdominals.

*Stop looking. Jeez, Vincent, perv much?*

What the hell had gotten into me? I'd managed to go almost twenty years without ogling. Why was he any different?

"Tell me about football," I said, moving to my bed. I sat cross-legged and pulled my pillow into my lap. Not to hide anything, just for something to hold. A barrier, a safety net. I needed a distraction from that sliver of skin above his waistband, and I figured getting Cobey to talk about football was my best bet.

"Football? What do you wanna know?"

"What you do on the field. What position you play and what that means."

He sat up, smiling now. "I'm a middle linebacker."

That name meant absolutely nothing to me. "And what does a middle linebacker do? If I'm going to watch a game on Saturday, then I should probably have some kind of inkling of what's going on."

And that was when I got to see the real Cobey Green.

He was animated, used his hands when he talked, his eyes lit up. Actually, his whole face lit up. He talked about defensive lines and offensive centers, stopping the run, the pass, and everything in between. He talked about scoping out the whole game, watching for any plays that develop and directing his team accordingly. He spoke of things I didn't understand and had never heard of.

But he spoke with such passion it was hard not to be enthralled. For anyone to be that passionate about their chosen career . . . well, it made me happy. Now, I'd never given football much thought before. Lord knows I'd never watched it. Throughout most of my school days I'd been at the butt end of too many jock's jokes to want to avoid football players forever.

But Cobey wasn't like that.

Well, I didn't think he was. Maybe seeing him on the football field or with his football friends might change all that. I hoped it didn't change him because, holy hell, he was so attractive and sweet—

"So do you want one pass to get into the game or two," he asked. I must have zoned out because his question took me by surprise.

"Oh, just one is fine."

"No plus one? I know you said before you didn't have a boyfriend but that doesn't mean you're not seeing someone. If you want them to come along, that's totally fine . . . if you have a secret boyfriend or something and just didn't want me to know."

"No, there's no secret boyfriend." I felt my cheeks burn. And there he was, sitting across from me, all attractive and whatever, with that tell-me-all-your-secrets face.

So I did.

"There's no not-secret boyfriend either. I've, uh, never had a boyfriend of any kind. Secret or otherwise."

He smiled. "Really?"

Regret and embarrassment sank in my belly. "Is that funny? Smiling at someone when they—"

"No, no!" he said quickly, sitting forward on his bed and reaching his hand over to pat my knee. "I'm not smiling at you. I just . . . I thought you'd have a boyfriend for sure and you just didn't want to tell me the other day. Because you're not out, and I thought maybe he's not either and you were protecting him. I would totally respect that."

I shook my head, undecided on how to feel. "Nope. Never had a boyfriend."

"That's totally cool," he said.

I snorted. "I beg to differ. It's not that I don't want to. It's just that I'm busy, and I've always been busy. I spent my entire high school years trying to avoid being gay, so I'd study and study some more. Can't be thinking about kissing boys when you're thinking about quantum physics, right?"

"Uh, I was absolutely the kissing-boys type. Not so big on the quantum thing. And girls. I was kissing them too."

God, there he was having the best of both worlds and I hadn't even kissed anyone.

"Maybe this explains why I'm failing class," he said with a smirk.

"Well, it probably explains why I've always made the dean's list and am still a virgin."

Cobey stared.

Did I say that out loud? Did I just tell the most popular guy at school that I was a virgin? Oh sweet mother of god. *Did I just say that . . . ? Did I just . . .*

"Virgin?"

*Yes, I did.*

I pressed my pillow into my face. "I meant a virgin when it

came to girls. Can we just pretend I never said anything? Why do I keep spilling out all this shit to you?"

A few seconds later, the pillow gently tugged away and Cobey's face was on the other side of it, all compassion and understanding. "It's okay, Vincent."

I wanted to die, but apparently all I could manage was groaning and burying my face in my hands. "God, can we just pretend I never said anything?"

This time he peeled back my fingers. "Don't be embarrassed. It's completely cool. Not everyone has had sex by now. Some people don't ever want to have sex."

"I do," I blurted out because I wasn't embarrassed enough. "I just haven't found . . . I mean, I'm really bad at social interaction. Of any kind. Like this would be Exhibit A in a very long list of documentary evidence."

He chuckled, and it was only then that I realized he still had hold of my hand.

## COBEY

Holy shit, Vincent was so freaking adorable. And hot. How could someone be adorable and hot at the same time? Like that didn't make sense.

And having a conversation with him was fun.

That didn't make sense either. How could it be *fun*?

He spoke so well, and I was sure he probably dumbed down his word-choice when he was talking to me, but he listened when I spoke. He *really* listened. Fully invested like I was saying the most intelligent stuff he'd ever heard. No one treated me like I was smart.

And that was sexy as hell.

He was sexy as hell.

And he was a virgin.

I had absolutely zero problem with that. As a matter of fact, I even respected him for telling me.

"I just keep blurting shit out to you," he said. His cheeks were red and he kept trying to hide his face, so I held his hand. Then he covered his eyes with his other hand, so I held that one too.

I was still sitting on the edge of my bed, him on his, but I could easily reach him. "I told ya," I replied, aiming for a joke. "I got a face that people spill random shit to. It happens all the time so it's absolutely not your fault. It's my face's fault."

He eventually smiled. "Your face is fine. Better than fine, actually. Very handsome." And he was back to looking horrified. "I mean, handsome by a classic definition. What a Greek sculptor would describe as masculine and symmetrical. And Christ, if I could just stop talking, that'd be great."

I chuckled. "No one's ever called my face symmetrical before."

"Well, of course they haven't. Because it's highly unlikely you've spoken to a socially inept loser before."

I squeezed both his hands. "You're not those things. And I'm taking the Greek sculptor thing as a compliment, so thanks."

"I'm sorry."

"Don't apologize." I wasn't sure how to bring this up, but I wanted to address it. So I went with blunt. "So about the virginity thing—"

"Oh my god, no, please don't. We were going to pretend I never said that, remember?"

"I just wanted to say it's cool and I respect you for telling me."

"Oh."

"Even though you said it's not really by choice."

"Well, I don't talk to people, if I can avoid it. And I believe actually speaking to a guy would be a requirement for us to actually . . . do anything."

"Talking helps, yes. You talk just fine with me," I pointed out.

"Because of your face. We've discussed this several times."

"Oh yes. My handsome and symmetrical face."

He squinted his eyes closed but he did laugh. "God."

"I can help you," I said. "With your guy problem."

Then his eyes almost popped right out of his head and his voice went up an octave. "You can . . . help me? Do what exactly? Have sex? My god! What does that even mean? Where would I even start?"

"What?"

"My guy problem," he said quickly. His eyes did this weird thing like he was trying to make me understand without him actually saying the words. When that didn't work, he whispered, "My virginity problem."

"Oh, no, well, I didn't mean that. But wow, is that where your mind went right out of the blocks? Because damn, Vincent. That's bold."

"No, I didn't . . . Well, I kind of did. But . . ." He closed his eyes tight. "For the love of god, can the universe rip open and swallow me whole. I'd even settle for a catastrophic cosmic event that ended all mankind on Earth right now just so I don't have to live through one more second of this mortifying conversation."

God, he cracked me up.

"What the hell is a catastrophic cosmic event?"

He looked at me then. "Solar flare. Asteroid collision. If the sun expands. Gamma ray energy bursts."

"Gamma rays. Like what happened to The Hulk?"

"Theoretically, that result is unlikely yet unproven, so—" He shook his head. "Maybe?"

"And um. Just out of curiosity, how likely is the sun to expand? Because that can't be good."

"It's not good. It would be the end, not just of Earth but of our solar system. And it's not technically *likely*."

"Well, good."

He made a face. "Actually, it's not likely, because it's inevitable. It's going to happen. In about seven billion years, so I don't think we'll need to worry."

"Jesus."

"Sorry."

"How does being that smart and knowing all that terrible shit not mess with your head?"

He shrugged. "It's fascinating to me. I've always loved science."

I was smiling at him, for no other reason than this was the best conversation I'd probably ever had, and he was being so cute and hot . . .

"I just wanna circle back for a sec," I said, because he'd said something earlier that I wanted to bring up. I didn't want to miss this opportunity.

"Oh god."

I chuckled. "Now you assumed I meant I would help with your virginity thing."

"There it is. I knew you were going to say that."

He tried to pull his hands away, but I held on. "Listen, listen. Don't be embarrassed. What I actually meant, and probably didn't explain very well, was that I could help you with talking to guys. Like practicing or whatever. That I would help socially, not sexually."

He rolled his eyes and mumbled something under his breath.

"Maybe get you out on some dates or something."

"I think I'd rather the sun expand and consume every planet in its path."

I laughed again. "My god, you're so funny. Any guy's gonna love you."

"You're forgetting one thing," he said. "That I'm not out. No one knows I'm gay, which is going to make dating a guy some-what difficult."

Ugh. Fair point.

"Well, that just means we have to do some low-key stuff until you're ready."

"Low-key stuff?"

"Yeah. Low-key. There's a lot of guys on campus who'd be up for some private time with the sexiest genius at school."

He stared. "Sexiest . . ."

"Hell the fuck yes, you are. Vincent, you are *fine.*"

His cheeks bloomed with red. "Yeah, no. Thanks anyway, but I don't want to just get thrown into some room with a random guy. That's not me. Actually, that makes me feel kinda nauseous."

Oh jeez.

I let go of his hands and sat beside him on his bed instead. "You okay?"

"Yeah, I just . . . I . . ." He ran his hand through his hair, making a strand fall into his eyes. "When I said I haven't done anything, I mean literally anything. It's embarrassing, and I know everyone else is out there having sex all the time, and I'm nineteen and I haven't even . . ."

"Not everyone is having sex all the time. And nineteen isn't old. There is no age cutoff. It has to be right for you." I took his hand again. "It's like you said to me about getting tutored. Some people just need some help with certain subjects. I need help with math, and you need help with meeting people."

He met my eyes. "Are you saying you'll tutor me in how not to be a social pariah?"

I grinned. "Yes! And believe me, it'll be easy as fuck. If you can hang out with any person and talk the way you're talking with me, you'll be just fine."

"It's not my ability to hold a conversation," he said quietly. "It's meeting new people. It's not really even being in a crowd; it's being the center of attention. But mostly meeting new people. And the thought of having to make small talk makes me want to vomit."

"Well then, I'll tutor you in the art of meeting new people and not vomiting on them if there's small talk."

"Oh great."

"Remember, you only have to meet new people once. Once you've met them the first time, you're no longer meeting new people."

He didn't look convinced.

I nudged his shoulder. "Oh, come on. It'll be fun. Then who knows. You might meet someone you want to meet a second time."

He looked over at me. "You're more excited about this than me."

"Yes, because I get to be the tutor. I've never been the smart one before."

He chuckled. "Okay then. But maybe I can tutor you with some math in return, like a trade."

"You will? I didn't think you were allowed. I don't want you getting into trouble."

"It'd just be between you and me. Rafe can't know."

"That would actually really help me out," I admitted. "Because I've tried reading that stupid calculus introduction six times and I can't make sense of it."

He smiled and nudged his shoulder to mine, the blush down his neck a rich pink. "It'll be fun."

# FOUR

## VINCENT

I COULDN'T BELIEVE this was happening.

Was I really going to have Cobey Green tutor me on how to not be a social pariah?

Yes, I was.

When he first mentioned it, I thought he meant he'd tutor me in sex.

I'd almost died.

I mean, I would have said yes.

I would have jumped at the chance. He was Cobey Green for god's sake. Body of a Greek god, totally gorgeous, and the best part? He was such a nice guy.

The nicest guy.

But getting back to the offer to help me be more sociable . . . he was also one of the most popular guys at school. If there was anyone who could help me deal with my inability to speak to people, it'd be him.

And the best part?

It meant we got to hang out more. Just us, in our room. Which yes, I knew that defeated the purpose of meeting *new* people, but the fact I wanted to spend time with *him* was a miracle in itself.

I could talk to him though. He was like no one else I'd ever known.

And—and this was the big one—he knew my secret and he didn't care. I'd never come out to anyone. Ever. I'd never felt safe enough. But Cobey was different. For whatever reason, I just found myself opening up to him like a freaking suitcase.

He knew I was gay, and it didn't change one thing between us. He was bisexual, so maybe it was having another queer person to talk to that made me trust him. He relaxed me. I could be me around him.

I'd never had that before.

So hell yes, I was going to take him up on his offer of tutoring me in how not to be a loser. I sure as hell didn't mind running him through some calculus as some kind of trade-off.

And the next day, it was all I could think about.

We'd agreed to keep it kind of casual, no pressure. If one of us had another obligation one night, we'd understand. And if one of us felt uncomfortable at all, about anything, and wanted to end the agreement, we'd both agreed to end the arrangement and never talk about it again.

He had a weight-training session and I had two tutoring sessions, so we both weren't getting back to the room super early anyway. Which was probably a good thing, so I wasn't sitting at my desk waiting anxiously for him to get back like a loser.

Well, I wasn't sitting there waiting for long anyway.

He burst into the room, all grinning and clean-smelling. He dumped his gym bag at the foot of his bed. "Come on, on your feet, soldier," he said, pulling my chair out. "I'm starving."

"Oh, okay," I said, standing up. "I wasn't expecting you back so soon."

That was a lie. I'd had one eye on the door for the last twenty minutes.

We started down the corridor to the dining hall. "I showered at the gym," he said.

"Ugh, like high school?" I grimaced. "That was horrifying. In the top five worst parts of all schooling experiences."

"In the top five worst? It was in the top five best for me. Got my first hand job in—"

I tripped over my feet and he caught me. "Jesus."

He laughed. "His name was Cameron Daniels. Played wide receiver on our high school team."

"I think you and I had very different high school experiences."

"Didn't enjoy it?"

"Well, let's just say I'll be able to skip orientation day in hell."

He snorted and held the door to the dining hall for me. "After you."

*Christ, don't blush, Vincent. Have some decorum.*

"I thought we were going to start on our tutorial thing," I said, then regretted it immediately.

*Good one, Vincent. We agreed no pressure and you're being a whiney bitch before day one.*

"We are starting," he said, still grinning as we got our meals.

I looked around at the mostly busy tables. "In the dining hall? Oh please, dear god, don't tell me you've arranged some social get-acquainted game with strangers because honestly, I would rather be back in high school."

He was momentarily confused. "What? Oh no, no. I wasn't kidding when I said I was starving. I haven't eaten since lunch and Coach busted my ass all afternoon, so the dinner thing was no lie. I need food. But I was thinking we should start your lessons at the very beginning."

"Oh dear god. This sounds ominous. Why am I scared?"

He put his plate down at a table, then put his big hand on top of my shoulder and gave me a squeeze. "I would never throw you into the deep end or do anything that'd make you feel bad."

I sagged into the seat opposite him. "Thank god. So what did you mean by the very beginning?"

"Where all conversations should start when it comes to dating."

I felt like I was waiting for a punchline. I was almost too scared to ask. "Oh yeah? And what's that?"

"Respect."

I was not expecting that.

"We're going to talk about respect?"

"Absolutely. The respect for yourself and your body."

I waited for him to smile, waited for him to say *ha ha, gotcha,* as if it was some kind of joke. But no, he was actually serious. He wasn't kidding when he said he was starving, either. He shoveled in a few mouthfuls of lasagna. His plate was loaded with pasta and salad, easily double mine.

"Respect," I mumbled, still not quite believing it, and put my breadstick on the edge of his plate.

He nodded as he swallowed, then picked up the breadstick. "Thanks."

"You're welcome."

He smiled as he bit into it. "Respecting yourself is important," he said, then added a forkful of lasagna to his mouthful. He waved his fork as he chewed and swallowed. "So is setting boundaries and knowing what you want and what you don't."

I wasn't quite following. "Are we talking about being sociable?"

"Yes. And dating. And possibly sex."

I dropped my fork. Then I looked around to see if anyone had heard us. It hadn't appeared that anyone was listening. No one was gawking at us anyway.

Thank god.

"Uh, I didn't realize that was part of my tutoring," I said, almost certain my face was close to catching fire.

Cobey just grinned and ate some salad. "I think it's a step-by-step thing. Like in my weight-training session today, I was thinking. When I was starting out, I had an end goal in mind, right? I wanted to be able to bench 200 pounds. That was my end goal.

But I couldn't just start at 200. I needed to start smaller, adding increments when I was ready."

"I think I can see where this is going."

"Right. So let's pretend that sex is 200 pounds."

"That's what I thought."

"And you're starting at the very beginning. So if we're adding weights, you're starting at what, five pounds?"

"Uh no. There's been no adding of weights, probably just the bar by itself. The weights are still in the packaging. Brand-new. Never been . . . used."

He laughed. "Okay, so starting with just the bar is what everyone starts with. Some people are very happy to never add any weights at all. They have no desire to add any weights. And that's cool. Kudos to them."

This analogy was kinda cute.

"Some people want to get to 200 in their first session, and"—he shrugged—"sometimes it works out okay. Sometimes it ends badly."

"Did you?" I asked. "Get to 200 in your first session?"

He shook his head. "No. Started with smaller weights first."

"So, just out of curiosity and for a point of reference, was the Cameron Daniel's experience a ten-pound increment or a twenty-pound increment?"

He laughed again, loud enough that a few people turned their heads. "Holy shit, you are so funny. But that was definitely a twenty-pound increment." Then he leaned in and spoke in a whisper. "Having another guy's hand on your dick for the first time is a big deal."

*Fucking hell.*

Embarrassed and turned on. Not a good combination.

"I'm sure it is," I said, my voice cracking.

He kept eating while I tried not to die. Or get a full-on erection.

"So," he said, ever so casually. "What's your end goal? What limit of weights do you eventually want to be able to bench press? Not right now, but end goal."

Oh my god.

"Uhhh." I cleared my throat and tried again. "Best-case scenario, long-term goal, would be 200 pounds. Even though the idea of that kind of scares me. And at this point in my life, I'd be happy with starting with five-pound weights."

He grinned. "Perfect. That's what I'm here for. I'm going to be your personal trainer slash tutor. I'll help you get there." Then he stopped, his eyes going wide. "Oh, I mean, I'll help you be ready to lift weights with someone else. Not me, if you know what I mean. I'm not implying *that* kind of one-on-one personal training . . ." He leaned in again, a worried look on his face, and he whispered, "I mean, I'll help you be ready in theory, for when you find someone you want to lift weights with."

Even though it was all kinds of mortifying, I couldn't help but smile at how cute he was. In a giant-football-player kind of way.

He ate the last of his lasagna. "So the first five-pound weight-lifting session," he said, then took a sip of his water. "Respect yourself and your body. There will always be some guys at the weight-lifting station who will try and pressure you into lifting way more than what you're ready for. You need to know what you're comfortable lifting, and you need to tell them to fuck off if they're dicks about it."

Could he be any sweeter?

"Thank you. I appreciate that."

"You're very welcome." He looked at my plate. "You need to eat more."

I stabbed some lasagna. "Sorry. I've been sitting here trying not to die of embarrassment."

He chuckled. "It's nothing to be embarrassed about. You wait till we get to the health routines of the weight-lifting-equipment conversation."

"Oh my god."

He sighed happily. "We have some other tutorials to get

through first. More about the social stuff and meeting new people. Which I know is what we agreed on. But there I was, thinking about you having never lifted *any* weights before—"

"Oh god."

"—or done any kind of weight training at all, ever."

"Yes, thanks for bringing that up, twice."

"I mean, lifting 200 pounds is awesome, but honestly, every five-pound increment along the way is great too. And they're important and can sometimes be more rewarding. I figured the meeting-new-people thing might lead to the beginning of some weight lifting, and I thought maybe I could offer some advice before you try to lift something you're not ready for."

I sighed, studying the honest concern on his face, and I smiled. It was hard not to smile at him. "That's actually sweet of you. And even though it's mortifying, I do appreciate it."

He put his hand to his heart and sighed. "Awesome. I thought you might be mad. Did you like the weight-lifting metaphor?"

"It's great."

"I made a real effort not to use the lifting phrase *clean and jerk*."

"Clean and what?"

He laughed. "It's a lifting technique. But that's why I didn't use it."

"I'm grateful." Because god, who named it that? "Can I ask you something?"

"Sure."

"Can you actually lift 200 pounds?"

He grinned. "I have a PB of 235."

"Holy shit."

"How much can you lift?"

"Me? Lift weights? Uh, in the metaphor and in real life, the answer is just the bar. Not that I've ever tried to lift actual weights, not since PE in high school, anyway." Which was something I tried very hard not to remember. "But I can carry around six textbooks all day, does that count?"

"It should. Those fuckers are heavy."

I laughed just as someone came up to the table. He was a fit, good-looking guy. A senior, I thought. "Hey, Green, good luck on Saturday."

Cobey gave him the same killer grin he gave everyone. "Thanks, man."

They did some bro-handshake thing. I assumed he was a foot-ball buddy.

"You gonna come watch?" Cobey asked.

Oh, okay then, so maybe not a football buddy.

"Yeah, yeah. Me and a few of the guys were gonna go. Catch you at the bar afterwards?"

Cobey nodded. "Win or lose."

The guy left, and as soon as he was out of earshot, Cobey leaned in again. "Okay, we need to set some guidelines."

"Guidelines for what?" Jesus, did he mean guidelines for being in public? "If you don't want to sit with me . . ."

He blinked. God, was he offended. "The fuck?"

My eyes met his. "Guidelines," I replied, gesturing to the other people. "For being seen with you . . ."

His jaw bulged and he stared. "Okay, listen up, my guy, I'm only gonna say this once."

*Shit.*

*I think I just made Cobey Green mad.*

He raised one eyebrow, his eyes like lasers. "I'm sitting with you, talking to you, I'm friends with you, and I don't give one flying fuck what anyone else thinks." He wasn't smiling. The easy-going Cobey was gone. "When have I ever given you the impression that I'm a snob?"

"Well, never—"

"That's right. Never. Because I'm not. And I know you worry about meeting new people, which is what I wanted the guidelines on. If it was okay to introduce you or if you're not comfortable with that."

"Oh."

"Jesus, you thought I was embarrassed to be seen with you?"

I shrugged. "Maybe."

He sighed, long and loud. "Right then. Looks like I need to add another lesson on self-respect into our little tutor exchange."

"Another lesson on self-respect? For me?" I snorted. "Freud himself would need about ten lessons to put a dent in this disaster, just so you know."

He shook his head. "Vincent, Vincent, Vincent."

"Sorry. For thinking bad of you. I know you're not a snob. You're actually the nicest guy I think I've ever met. Every person on the planet likes you, and you speak to everyone, even if it's just to say hi. A snob would never do that."

"I can tell you a thing or two about snobs. I play football, have my whole life. I've seen my share of douchey egos and shitty attitudes to last a lifetime. It's ugly as fuck."

"That jock superiority complex," I mumbled. "I've seen enough of that to last me a lifetime too."

"High school?"

I nodded. "Nothing terrible, but not fun, either."

He gave me a sympathetic smile. "Come on, I want iced coffee. My treat. If you're going to torture me with math later, I'll need some caffeine and sugar."

"Oh yes, torture by an introduction to trigonometric functions."

He grimaced. "My god, do you hate me *that* much?"

I laughed. "I don't hate you at all."

## COBEY

Vincent was like one of those wooden knot puzzles that sat on the shelf in my dad's home office. A complete package to look at when it was all together, but its parts were complex and difficult to assemble.

I knew the reason he assumed I was embarrassed to be seen with him had nothing to do with me, and everything to do with how he saw himself.

Which was obviously with his eyes closed.

Because he was a complete package.

Genuine, considerate, funny, smart, and gorgeous.

And he was all I could think about. Since yesterday, with our first 'tutoring' session where I explained the weight-lifting thing, he was *all* I could think about. We'd gone to the coffee shop after dinner. I wanted to see how he handled a social setting that wasn't the dining hall. He was fine, of course. We chatted and he was his usual funny self, but he looked around a lot, didn't make eye contact with anyone else but me, and was very happy to leave when I suggested we go.

And yeah, I didn't even mind the trigonometry intro he put me through. He even explained some of it in ways I could understand. Almost.

But he was in the shower when I woke up and he was gone by the time I came back to the room. I thought he might have been avoiding me, but I ran into him in the dining hall. He had his books in one hand and a coffee in his other, and a croissant in his mouth as he struggled with the door.

"Hey," I said, holding the door for him.

"M-heh," he mumbled around the croissant.

I took the books from under his arm. "Let me get these for you."

"Oh." I wasn't sure if he blushed or if it was just the morning sun. He pulled the croissant out of his mouth. "Thanks."

"You late somewhere?"

"Ah yeah, I have a thing . . ." He glanced across the quad. "It's just a tutor briefing thing."

"Oh." *Thank god, because I thought he was avoiding me.* "I can carry these for you."

"No need. I don't want to be a bother . . ."

I grinned at him and started in the direction of the library. "You're no bother, Vincent."

He hurried to fall into step beside me. "Oh, I just . . ."

"Don't stress. I won't say anything to Rafe. Our agreement is just between us, right?"

"Our agreement? You make it sound like a . . . like a thing. I don't know, a sordid, secret thing."

I pushed the door open and held it for him with my foot. "It *is* a secret thing. But it's not sordid. Yet." *Unless you want it to be.* I shrugged to hopefully come off like I didn't care either way. "I mean, we haven't gotten to the heavy weightlifting part yet."

Aaaand that time he blushed. His cheeks went red and it spilled down his neck like ink in water.

It was so hot.

Fuck.

He fixed his glasses. "I, uh, I, um . . ."

"Hey Vincent," Rafe said as he came through the library. Then he looked at me as he opened the door to the tutoring center and went in. "Cobey, right?"

"Yep. That's me." I grinned at him, and again I held the door for Vincent with my foot.

He ducked his head as he passed me, his cheeks still flushed. Rafe put his things on his desk, and before he could ask any questions about finding a tutor, I put Vincent's books on the closest desk. "Don't mind me. I'm just here for the heavy lifting."

Vincent's eyes went to mine. And while I meant it as a joke, I realized now how it sounded.

"I mean, not just the heavy lifting. All kinds of lifting is important. All the small increments. Equally important."

Vincent stared. "Oh my god."

Rafe looked between us. "Is lifting weights a metaphor for something?"

"No," Vincent said quickly.

"Maybe," I added. "What's a metaphor?"

I was just kidding. I knew what a metaphor was. I laughed at

Vincent's expression and I backed out of the room. "Oh, Vincent," I said. "I have practice this afternoon and then I'll be at Shenanigans with the guys. It's what we normally do, and I'll probably eat there. But I'll see you after."

Vincent stammered and damn, if he didn't blush again. Rafe was still watching both of us, and I walked back across the quad to the dining hall with the biggest smile.

And all day in class, he was all I could think about.

That blush, that smile.

At practice too. Not that I missed any hits and my times were all good, but I couldn't help but think of something. There was something I didn't quite understand . . .

And only one person I could ask about it. In private and away from the whole team, preferably. But I was late hitting the showers after practice because I had to track down the admission pass for Vincent so he could come to the game tomorrow, which meant I didn't have a chance to catch Nate before we got to a crowded Shenanigans.

Nate Schumacher was a good friend of mine. He was a cornerback, fast as the wind, and probably one of the quieter guys on the team. He was smart too, and he was studying to be a social worker for kids. If the football thing didn't work out, that was.

"Here he is," Nate said as I finally got through the small talk with every person I had to pass on my way through. There was a group of five other teammates with him. "We're just about to order some food. Want in?"

"Hell yes."

We ordered and ate dinner, had another round of drinks, and I was there probably later than I wanted to be, but eventually when the others were gone, I had a chance to have a word in private.

"Can I ask you something?"

"Sure thing," Nate said. "You've been waiting all night to say something, so out with it."

I breathed out a laugh, trying to hide my nerves. "It's kinda weird, and I dunno if you can help me. It's probably stupid."

"What's up?"

"Well, I have a friend . . ."

He smiled. "Yes."

"No, it really is a friend. It's not me."

"Okay."

"Anyway, I'll try and make it quick. Me and this friend, we get along well. Really well, actually. But we're very different. In probably every way." I looked around the bar, which was full of my teammates, being loud as per usual. "And . . . I dunno, it's hard to explain. I was thinking today that yeah, we're really very different and I was thinking about why."

He tilted his head. "Okay. But being different can be a good thing."

"Oh yeah, it is for me and . . . this person. I think. But I don't know." I looked around the bar again, realizing I wasn't entirely sure what I wanted to know. "Never mind. It's stupid. I don't even know what I'm talking about."

His eyes met mine and he smiled. "You like this person."

Well, fuck. "Yeah, I guess. It's all kind of new."

"And you can't figure them out because they're not like one of your teammates?"

Even though what I really wanted to ask was more than just that, Nate wasn't far off. I snorted. "You're good at this."

He smiled. "But if you're after relationship advice, I don't know if I'm much help."

"No, it's more of a psychology question," I replied. "I think. So *I* can figure out the relationship part. But I dunno. It sounded better in my head because I ain't saying that shit out loud."

Nate gave me a kind smile. "Sure you don't want to just say it?"

I shook my head. "Nah. Thanks anyway. I'll figure it out . . . or I could just do the mature thing and ask my friend for the truth. I just wanted an understanding before I did, but maybe I'm way off. Overthinking shit. Sorry, ignore me."

"Overthinking because you like this person."

"Yeah, I said that already."

"No, you *like* like them. Have never seen you bent outta shape over anyone before."

"I'm not bent out of shape. I'm just . . . It's fun and different, and I might be using the guise of helping them in exchange for spending time with them and maybe some making out if it gets to that. Okay, it's so I can maybe make out with them, and maybe more, in exchange for—"

"Okay, I'm gonna stop you right there."

"What? Is it bad? Does it sound terrible?"

"Is it consensual?"

"What?" I recoiled. "God, yes. Of course yes. I would never . . ."

"Is the exchange equal? Is it fair to both parties?"

"Yes," I replied. Jeez, he made it sound like it was a bad, bad thing. I mean, I thought it was equal . . . but I hadn't asked Vincent if he thought that. "I think so?"

"You need to ask them, and you need to tell them your intentions. Honesty is the best policy, and there should be no secret guises, dude. Consent can change at any time. Always make sure both parties are happy with the exchange at all times. You have some arrangement for helping each other but you have intentions they're not aware of."

Jesus. This wasn't even what I was going to ask him, but he'd given me a bit to think about.

"Does that help?" he asked.

"Uh, sure. Yeah. I think. I mean, it wasn't what I came here to ask you, but it's a good point."

God. Now I was even more confused.

"What did you come here to ask me?"

"Oh, it doesn't matter. It was just about self-esteem and how to understand why someone doesn't seem to have any. But I think I have other issues to address first."

Nate's expression changed, softened somehow. "You're one of the good ones, Cobey." He offered me a fist bump.

"If I'm one of the good ones, then why do I feel like shit?"

"You feel like shit because you're one of the good ones."

I wasn't sure I understood that, but okay.

"I better go," I said. "I have some shitty feelings to fix."

Nate smiled. "See you tomorrow. Have your head in the game, okay? We need all of you on that field tomorrow."

I quietly slipped out of the bar, no goodbyes, no small talk, and jogged back to the dorm. I practiced in my head what I was going to say to him. That consent was important and I was wrong and I'm sorry. I'd make it clear and to the point and leave the ball in his court. I repeated it over and over to make sure I got it right.

It was late and most of the lights were off, but I took the stairs two at a time to our floor and unlocked our door. "Hey, Vincent?"

The lights were off.

Shit.

He sat up on his bed and switched on his reading light. He put his glasses on and squinted at me. "What's wrong?"

I sat on my bed. "Uh, nothing really. Sorry to wake you, but I . . . but this is kinda important."

Vincent ran a hand through his bed hair and squinted some more. "Uh, okay."

I took a deep breath. *Just say it exactly like you practiced . . .*

*Here goes nothing.*

"I put weight lifting on the table without your consent because I thought maybe I'd get to kiss you, which I can see now was wrong, and I should have been upfront about my intentions but I wasn't, and that put my balls in your court and now I'm a terrible person."

Vincent stared at me for a long second, then he blinked. "I'm sorry. You put your balls where?"

# FIVE

## VINCENT

MY BRAIN DIDN'T FUNCTION OVERLY well when I was woken up at the best of times, but I replayed in my mind what Cobey had blurted out and I still couldn't connect the dots.

Something about his balls.

Now he looked all kinds of horrified. "My balls . . . ? No, no, I'm sorry. God, this is embarrassing. I meant to say my ball was in your court. Is that how the saying goes?"

I scrubbed my hand over my face. "Something like that. So there was no plural?"

"Nope. Only have a singular ball here." Then his eyes went comically wide. "I mean, I have two. Definitely have two . . . last time I checked—oh my god, can we start this conversation over?"

"I'm not sure this conversation ever really got started, to be honest."

"Yeah, I practiced what to say when I ran here, but then my nerves fucked it all up."

"Your nerves?" What did Cobey Green ever have to be nervous about?

He put his hand to his heart and looked a mix of hopeful and disappointed. "Did you not hear the first part of what I said?"

I had to think . . .

*I put weight lifting on the table without your consent because I thought maybe I'd get to kiss you.*

Oh my god.

"You . . . you . . . want to kiss me?"

I was certainly awake now.

He laughed. Not in a mocking way but an embarrassed way. "Crap. Well, yes. Speaking of weight-lifting increments, I thought maybe it was something that might possibly eventually happen? Once we'd already built up some weight increases. There'd be other things too, like hand holding, but yeah, kissing is fun. Like I said, all the small weight increments are important, and I'm not talking about diving right into the big 200-pound deadlift. I mean, that's a lot of fun too. But god, I'm getting this so wrong. I ran back from Shenanigans because I spoke to Nate and he basically said what I was doing wasn't consensual, and it freaked me out . . . well, he didn't say it wasn't consensual. He asked me if I thought it was—"

"Who is Nate?"

"Nate Schumacher. He's a friend of mine, on the team—"

"And you told him about me?"

He looked kinda panicked. "Oh no. No names. I didn't even say if it was a guy or girl. I just said there was something I wanted to ask him. He's studying to be a social worker or a shrink or something, and he's super smart. Not as smart as you, but still way smarter than me. Anyway, I wanted to ask him about trying to understand someone who is different from me, in a lot of ways, because I like them and didn't want to fuck it up. Which is stupid because look at me now. Doing a spectacular job of that."

"Cobey, are you okay?"

"Not really. Anyway, then I said to Nate that I'd kind of set up a mutual deal with this person for us to help each other—I didn't mention tutoring, so it's fine—but I did say that maybe I'd kind of sneakily added weight-lifting to the deal, and he was like, 'Holy shit, dude, if they didn't agree to that then that's not cool.'"

I was finally catching up.

He put his hand back to his heart. "I swear I didn't mean to pressure you or to blindside you with the whole weight-lifting thing, and I didn't mean to make you feel obligated. You said you'd never lifted weights before and I respect that. You certainly don't have to do anything you don't want to do, and to think for one second that I might have pushed you into a corner . . ." He put his hand to his stomach and made a face. "Well, it makes me feel kinda sick."

"Okay, first up, Cobey, it's fine. Relax. Please don't vomit. I'm a sympathetic vomiter, and if you hurl, then I'll hurl and it'll be awful for everyone. And secondly," I said as I pulled my blankets up, "you did ask me if it was okay, about adding weight lifting to our *agreement*."

"I did? I was so nervous I don't really remember . . ."

"You asked me twice, I think."

He sagged with relief. "Phew. Jesus. I really freaked out."

"I can tell."

"But just so we're clear, you're okay with it? I mean, if things were to . . ." He cringed. "Fuck, it sounds so bad. What I mean to say, and full disclosure here, just gonna put myself out here . . ." He let out a breath. "I would like to help you socialize more and meet new people. That still stands. Because that includes hanging out, which I'm all for. And if you do want to add weight increments, then maybe making out, and I'd be all for that too. Only if you're okay with that, and only if you absolutely want to do that too. If you don't, that's totally fine. God, this has been a lot, I'm sorry."

I couldn't help but smile because, oh my freaking god, Cobey Green was saying all this to me.

To. My. Face.

"Um, well, it *is* a lot," I agreed. "But I'm okay with that. If you're okay with that. With the socializing part, and the . . . other part." My face started to burn from the inside.

Cobey was smiling now. "I'm definitely okay with that."

"Although, full disclaimer, or more of a reminder, that there are exactly no weights on my weight-lifting bar."

"That's fine. Small steps, remember?"

I don't think he understood. "When I told you I haven't done anything, I meant none. I have no experience. In anything. And I mean *anything*, Cobey. I've never even kissed a guy before. I've held hands with a guy. Once. And that was with you the other night."

He blinked in surprise. "Me? When I held your hand?"

I nodded, trying not to die inside. "Uh, yeah."

A slow smile pulled at his lips and he cautiously got up and sat on the edge of my bed.

Holy shit.

He held out his hand, palm up. Not entirely sure what he wanted me to do with it, and not entirely sure my heart or lungs were functioning properly, I gave him my hand.

He threaded our fingers and let our joined hands fall to the bed between us, and he grinned. "Now you've done it two times. You're a pro at this."

I laughed because, oh my freaking god.

I was holding hands with Cobey Green.

"You can do things like this," he said, taking my hand in his but holding mine palm up. He looked at it and trailed his fingers down mine. "Feel it, study it."

Oh holy hell.

But, like a good student, I took his hand and let my fingers skim over his knuckles, his palm, his fingers. Our hands were very different. His was huge; mine was small by comparison. My fingers were slender; his were thicker—good for playing football, I guessed. My hands were soft; his had callouses.

"From doing weights," he said as I touched the rough patches of skin below his little and ring finger. "And I mean actual weights, in the gym at training. Not our codeword for weights. To have callouses from that would be weird."

I chuckled. "Thanks for clarifying." I put my palm to his. I laced our fingers. I explored the feel, the warmth.

"How does it feel?" he murmured.

I looked at his face instead of our hands, ignoring the timbre of his voice. "Oh, um . . . it feels kinda great."

"It does, doesn't it? Like I said, the small steps are important. And a lot of fun." But then he took his hand back and rested it on his leg. I missed it already . . . "Now, I want you to be the one to take my hand first. Imagine I'm some guy you're dating and you want to hold his hand. You'll have to be the one to make the first move."

Was he serious?

I looked at his face, and yes, he was serious.

Oh god. How hard could it be?

I looked at his hand, which was on his knee. My hand was half a foot from his, but it might as well have been a mile.

So apparently it wasn't easy.

My stomach was in a giant greasy knot, my mouth was suddenly dry. And my heart was thumping painfully.

I reached out slowly but stopped just short. "Ah, Cobey?"

"Yeah?"

"M-may I hold your hand?"

He grinned, and maybe it was the dim lighting, but that smile . . . holy crap, he was so hot. "You may," he said. "Thank you for asking."

I slid my hand over his, relishing in the warmth, the feel, and slotted my fingers between his. My nerves settled a bit but my heart kept thrumming.

"Now about your first kiss . . ."

My heart just about stopped. "Oh my god."

He chuckled. "Not tonight. I just want to give you plenty of warning, that's all. Time to back out if you want."

I accidentally squeezed his hand. "I won't back out."

"So maybe tomorrow?" he said. "I have the game—"

"Oh."

"You sound disappointed."

"I am," I blurted out. I hadn't meant to say that out loud. "Not about football. About the waiting. I just wish I could just get rid of all the firsts; first kiss, first time. Just to have it over and done with, ya know? And not have it hanging over my head. I just don't know why interacting with people is so hard for me. Math, chemistry, physics, no problem. Being myself around people, talking to people . . ." I shook my head. "I can't do it."

Now it was Cobey who squeezed my hand. "You don't want to rush into anything you're not ready for."

"I am ready. Physically, I am ready." Like saying that wasn't embarrassing at all. "Except human interaction is different."

"You interact with me just fine."

"But you're different."

"How?"

"I can talk to you."

"What about your friend Rafe?"

"Well, I can talk to him, I guess. I might have, maybe, come out to him today—"

"You what?" Cobey pulled on my hand and practically bounced on my bed. "Vincent, that's huge! What happened?"

"It was more what I didn't say than what I did say." I sighed and ran my free hand through my hair. "After you left us in the library this morning, he was staring at me. I tried to pretend he wasn't, and I must have looked like I was having a stroke or something because then he asked if I was okay. I said of course I was. Then he said something similar to but not exactly, I'm paraphrasing here, 'Well, I think he likes you,' and at that point I almost did have a stroke, and he said there was nothing wrong with that, and I agreed there was nothing wrong with that. Then he said I should maybe put myself out there and I said I was working on it, and he asked if I was by chance working on it with you, and then I really did almost have a stroke, and he stared at me for a really long time and he smiled that smile. You know the one that says they know?"

Cobey nodded.

"But I didn't say it was you. Not that he would say anything anyway, but I'm pretty sure he knows I'm gay. And no one in my life knows, Cobey. Just you. And now maybe Rafe. So yeah, it's been a day."

Cobey now held my hand in both his, and he leaned in close, his eyes on mine. "Vincent, it's okay. Just take a deep breath."

I inhaled deeply and let it out slowly.

"Do you feel better now that he knows? Or worried?"

I shrugged. "A bit of both, I think. Relieved, but then all day I got more annoyed with myself that I didn't say it outright. I panicked and missed my one chance."

"There's no *one* chance, Vincent. Coming out is something you have to do a lot. New friends, new workplace, new bosses, people who missed it the first time."

"Oh my god, that's . . . that's terrible. Don't tell me that."

"Or," he said gently, "you don't have to tell anyone anything. The only people who need to know are those you intend to be intimate with and your doctor, you know, for medical reasons. But honestly, if you go to bed with a guy, chances are he's gonna know you're queer."

That made me smile. "I would hope so." I wasn't sure how he did it, but he made me feel better. "Thank you."

"You're very welcome."

But then he was quiet, still with the intense eyes, and the atmosphere between us changed. A buzz went through me that I wasn't sure was fear or excitement.

Maybe both.

He licked his lips and swallowed. "I know I said I'd wait until tomorrow, but Vincent, I'd really like to kiss you right now."

My heart squeezed and my belly swooped. "Oh."

"Would that be okay?" he whispered.

Ho. Lee. Shit.

I couldn't speak. I couldn't breathe. I somehow barely managed a nod.

He cupped my jaw with one hand, his touch gentle and warm, and his thumb stroked my chin.

My heart squeezed to the point of pain.

He inched closer, his eyes darting from mine to my lips. I couldn't move. Frozen, every synapse in my brain misfiring in all directions, devoid of all thought but of him, this moment, waiting, waiting . . .

He lifted my chin, slowly closed the distance between us, and ghosted his lips across mine.

I had no air. No thoughts. Just this . . . just him and this perfect moment.

Then he kissed me again, pressing harder this time, lips parted, soft and scorching hot. His lips covered mine, his hand still cradled my jaw, his other hand still holding mine.

Time stood still.

He pulled back, smiling. "Now that's a first kiss," he murmured.

*Breathe, Vincent.*

*Breathe.*

Still nothing.

*Vincent, you need air!*

I sucked back a breath. I was dizzy from lack of oxygen but also from that kiss. My heart was jumping, my lungs burning. My brain was still offline.

Cobey laughed. "You okay?"

"Um. Wow," I said.

He squeezed my hand, still grinning. "It's late. We should get some sleep. I've got a game tomorrow. Oh, that reminds me." He took out his wallet and pulled out a slip of paper. "This pass'll get you into the game. If you still wanna come watch me play."

My fingers took the ticket as if they weren't connected to my brain.

How was he managing to talk so coherently?

He kicked off his shoes and pulled off his shirt.

Lord.

Then, like he was a normally functioning human being, he got into bed, rolled over to face the wall, and pulled up the covers. "Night, Vincent."

I sat there, touching my fingers to my lips trying to recapture the sensation . . . and he just went to bed?

What the hell?

I threw my pillow at him. "How am I supposed to go to sleep now?"

He burst out laughing and threw my pillow back to me. Harder than I threw it to him, naturally.

"Ow."

He chuckled. "Want me to tuck you in?"

Yes.

"No," I lied. I shuffled down into my bed, pulled the covers up, and switched the reading light off. "Night."

He was quiet for a long while, and I lay there, grateful he couldn't see me touching my lips where his lips had been.

Then he spoke. "Are you still smiling?"

"No." It would have sounded more convincing if I didn't *sound* like I was smiling.

He laughed. "Me either."

I laughed too, and he was quiet again until his breathing evened out and I knew he was asleep. I stared at the ceiling, at the poster of Mary-Jesus Adam Driver, oscillating between smiling and trying not to laugh because I'd just had my first kiss.

With Cobey freaking Green.

I closed my eyes, but I wasn't sleeping anytime soon.

## COBEY

I'd kissed a lot of people. Okay, well, not a lot. But a decent amount of people. Both guys and girls, and I didn't have a preference between the two, if I was being completely honest. I liked them both equally, and I liked them for what they were, for the differences between them. I liked kissing girls because they were softer and smelled like flowers or fruit, something pretty. I liked the way they fit against me. And I liked guys because they were angular with hard lines and because they smelled of spice and sweat, and the stubble and demanding hands. I really liked how they fit against me too.

But kissing Vincent was different.

I don't even know how to explain it.

It was his first kiss. I wanted to make it special. I wanted it to be something he'd remember. That thrill, that buzz, the dizzying excitement. I also wanted it to be sweet and tender because . . . well, because Vincent deserved that.

Those were the things I wanted to give to him, but I wasn't expecting to get them in return.

The thrill, the buzz, the lightheaded excitement.

And it was just a kiss.

No tongue, no wandering hands, no making out, no grinding. Just a kiss.

A kiss that felt like my first, not his.

Was I in trouble? Hard to tell. Maybe. I think the real question was 'did I want to be in trouble?' over Vincent Brandt and the answer to that was yeah, I think I kinda did.

Was I mad about it?

Nope.

A little scared, maybe. Only because there were quite possibly feelings behind the excitement.

Or maybe there was excitement because there were quite possibly feelings. At any rate, I wasn't examining any of that too closely. I was just enjoying it.

Because why not?

That thrill, the buzz of electricity, was a fucking ride.

I woke up and even after scrolling my socials for a good while, Vincent was still sound asleep. So I hit the showers, hoping he'd be awake so we could grab some breakfast.

Not even me coming back into the room woke him up.

It wasn't until I dumped my gym bag on my bed and unzipped it that he stirred. "Oh, I'm sorry, I didn't mean to wake you," I said, lying through my teeth. I absolutely did mean it.

He sat up, one eye still squinted shut, his hair a mess. "Time is it?"

"Eight fifteen."

"Ugh."

"Sleep well?"

"Was awake till three."

I sat on my bed and smiled right at his grumpy-sleepy face. "Any reason?"

His eyes cut to mine and I could see the second he remembered . . . his blush was a dead giveaway. "Oh. Uh . . ."

I laughed. "I slept like a baby. Had the best dream too. We were on your bed and we were kissing and it was awesome, and then I had to wait for ages for you to wake up and get dressed so we could go and get some breakfast. Come on, I'm starving. And I gotta eat before nine on game day. Breakfast by nine, lunch by noon."

He was squinting at me but he smiled. "You were waiting for me?"

I put on my spoiled-brat whiney voice. "Come on, Vincent. I'm on a schedule and I'm hungry. Get your ass out of bed."

He groaned out a chuckle, threw back the covers, and got out of bed. He wore old black fitted sweatpants and a T-shirt that looked genuine vintage. He went to his drawers and opened the second drawer and then looked at me. "Uh . . ."

"As much as I'm down for a strip show, there's no time to change. I'm hungry, Vee."

"Vee?"

"Yeah. It's short for Vincent. Like I'm short on patience."

He looked down at what he was wearing. "I can't wear this to the dining hall . . ."

"Sure you can. You look great."

He squinted at me again. "If you're having trouble seeing, you can wear my glasses."

"I have zero trouble, my friend. But I know what you can wear." I plucked my hoodie off the end of my bed and gave it to him. "Put that on."

He held the hoodie and stared at me. "Have you lost your mind?"

"What's wrong with it? It's my FU Kings hoodie."

"It has your name on the back of it. With your football number. I'll look like your groupie. And it's four sizes too big for me."

"It'll be fine. And who the hell has groupies?"

"Uh, hello? Mr. Popular Football Star. You do."

"I do not. Please, can we go eat breakfast?" I picked up his high-top Converse. "Here."

"I can't wear those without socks."

I pulled at my hair. "Vincent."

"Okay, okay," he said. He pulled the hoodie on, then his shoes, no socks. He stood up straight and tried to fix the sleeves. "I look like a child."

"You look . . ." He actually looked really good. It was just my gray football hoodie with purple writing: Franklin U on the front, GREEN 33 on the back. Nothing flashy, and it *was* four sizes too big on him. But seeing him in my clothes . . . with my name on his back? "You look good."

He was about to protest, because that's what Vincent did, so I grabbed his arm and pulled him out the door. "Come on, Vee. I'm dying here."

He laughed as he tried to match my strides. "All right, all right."

I piled my breakfast tray with fruit and yogurt, eggs and bacon with toast, water and juice.

Vincent got coffee and one piece of toast.

He sat facing me, and I'd shoveled in half my eggs and bacon before I stopped to speak. "You don't eat enough," I said between mouthfuls.

"I eat plenty." He nodded to my plate. "Do you need to let the kitchen know in advance before you get here so they can prepare?"

I laughed. "I'm a growing boy."

He sipped his coffee. "One thing I learned about Cobey Green today," he said, "is that from the time he says he's hungry, there is a very small window of opportunity before he gets grouchy."

I finished off the bacon. "I wasn't grouchy."

"I'm wearing my pajamas, your hoodie, and shoes without socks."

I snorted and started on the yogurt. "I can't believe I said no to the strip show."

He blushed. "There would've been no strip show."

"Ah, Vee. I spend half my life in a locker room. I see guys in their jocks every day. Not saying that to see you wouldn't be special, unless you're not wearing any . . ."

The blush on his cheeks darkened and bloomed right down his neck.

The spoonful of yogurt in my hand forgotten, I stared at him. "Holy shit. You're not wearing any underwear," I mumbled. I leaned in across the table and whispered, "You're going commando right now?"

"Would you shut up?" he hissed at me.

Damn.

*Damn.*

That was so fucking hot. Just sitting right there across from me, free balling. Oh god, that also meant he slept . . . I sat back in my seat and shook my head, smiling. "I'm having the best visuals right now."

"Oh my god."

I wondered if his face could get any redder when he pulled the hood up and cinched the drawstrings so he looked like Kenny from *South Park*.

"It's gonna be a great day." I dug into my yogurt and fruit. "We're gonna win the game today, for sure."

"I beg your pardon?"

At least I think that's what he said. "I can't hear you," I said, trying not to grin too hard. "You'll have to loosen the hoodie part."

He undid it and slipped the hood back, leaned back in his seat, and let out a sigh. Apparently he was ignoring the free-ball conversation. "So what does your football routine look like?" he asked. "You said you have set times for eating before a game."

"Oh yeah, that's just my own thing. I have a big breakfast, then lunch will be a simple protein and a complex carbohydrate. Nothing too heavy: grilled chicken and plain pasta and a bit of salad is usually good. I get nervous pre-game so I'm best not having a brick in my belly, ya know?"

"There's a lot more to playing football than I realized," he said flatly.

"What do you mean?"

He shrugged. "I dunno. I just thought you trained and played. I'm aware there's a level of fitness and dedication. I just didn't realize that football dictates not only what you eat and drink, but when."

"Gotta put the right fuel in if you want to get the best mileage, right?"

"True. But it's also the practice and the hours you put in, seven days a week."

"It is."

"I admire that. I always thought football players were just big and loud, typically conceited and cliquey."

"Wow."

He almost smiled. "But you're not any of those things. Well, apart from the big part. So maybe I can allow that not all football players are that way."

"Gee, thanks. You can't tell me there aren't conceited and cliquey nerdy geniuses. There are assholes in all groups."

He made a thoughtful face. "True."

"Do you all go commando?"

He rolled his eyes. "Not that I'm aware of."

I chuckled and finished my juice. "The rest of my pre-game routine is to head to the stadium with the guys for warm up. It's a home game so it's easy. And the game starts at four, so you'll wanna get there around three thirty. Get a drink, find your seat, that kind of thing."

He grimaced. "And there will be a lot of people there, won't there?"

I nodded. I certainly wasn't going to tell him that the stadium would be packed. "You'll have fun, just you wait and see."

"Well, I'll be there. Can't guarantee I'll enjoy it."

I found myself smiling at him again. Or still. I wasn't sure which, and I didn't know why. "So what will you do all day? What's your plan?"

"I usually hit the library."

"The library? Spend all your free time there?"

He met my gaze and there was a shift in his eyes now. The humor was gone, and he was guarded. "Yes."

"Do you spend all your time in a library because you're a genius? Or are you a genius because you spend all your time in the library?" I was aiming for funny.

He didn't smile. Not a real one, anyway. But before I could say anything else, some girls walked past. "Hi, Cobey," they said, trying to be cute. Their eyes went to Vincent, but he kept his head down.

I'd really said something that upset him. *Goddammit, Cobey.*

"Good luck today," one of the girls said. "We'll be there cheering for you."

"Thanks," I replied.

And then some guys sat two tables over. "Hey, Cobey, gonna smash them Dolphins today?"

I gave them a smile. "That's the plan."

I noticed them giving Vincent an up and down, and yeah, maybe him wearing my hoodie hadn't been a great idea . . .

"You ready to go?" I asked.

He gave a nod and stood up, and we never spoke all the way back to our room.

As soon as the door was closed, he pulled the hoodie off by the hem, lifting his T-shirt a bit as well. I saw his pale waist, slim and —god, I wanted to touch it, lick it . . .

He handed the hoodie back to me, startling me out of my dirty thoughts.

"Hey, Vee, if I said anything that upset you . . ."

He sat on his bed and pulled off his shoes. "No, it's fine. I just didn't like how everyone was staring at me."

Hmm. I wasn't sure I believed that.

"I didn't mean anything about you going to the library," I said. "It's great that you go there. They have excellent resources." Not that I'd really spent much time in one . . .

Vincent put his Converse on the floor, making sure they were perfectly neat. "For as long as I can remember, since I was really little, I would be at my local library most days. Every day, actually," he said, his voice quiet. "Growing up, it was just me and my dad and he wasn't around much, so the library was a safe place for me to go. It was open all the time, and it was free."

My heart sank to my feet. "Oh, Vincent, I'm sorry. I didn't know. I shouldn't have joked about that. I was just trying to make you smile."

"It's okay," he murmured, but the look on his face said it was anything but.

I wanted to go to him. I wanted to hug him until he felt better. Or until I did. But mostly him. Definitely him. I put my hand out and pulled it back just as quick. "Uh . . ."

He looked up at me. "What's wrong?"

I winced and maybe whined a bit. "I'm sorry. I don't know what to do. I made you feel bad and I want to hug you, but we haven't discussed that and I don't want to cross a line, and asking outright would probably sound weird, and I don't want to make it more awkward than I already have."

He gave me a sad smile. "It's fine, Cobey."

Oh, thank god.

I took his hand and pulled him to his feet and into my arms. He froze, rigid against me. "I meant it was fine, as in not awkward," he said. "Not fine for you to hug me."

I pulled back. "Shit. I'm sorry."

He laughed, his cheeks red. "Um, it's fine."

"Fine? Fine for what? As in not awkward, or was the hug fine? Because now I'm even more confused—"

"Well, it wasn't awkward," he said. "But now I'm not sure. And the hug was fine. As far as hugs go. Not that I'd know. Never really hugged anyone . . ."

"You've never hugged anyone?"

He shook his head. "Nope. It was nice."

Oh.

"Can I . . . ? Did you want . . . ? Would you . . . ?"

God, why was it so hard to ask?

He understood and nodded.

This time, I pulled him in slower, gently sliding my arms around him, my hands on his back. He was a lot smaller than me, in height and build, but he fit against me so well, his face pressed to my collarbone, his hands at my waist.

He breathed in deep and exhaled into the embrace.

"Hugs are good, right?" I asked.

"Mm." And for a few long seconds, he allowed himself to be hugged. Until he pulled away. "Oh." Then he very quickly sat on his bed. His cheeks red, his eyes wide.

"What happened?" I asked, noticing he was sitting awkward, kinda leaning forward. Aaaand then the penny dropped. I sat on the edge of my bed. "Oh."

"You can stop smiling. It's not funny."

"It kinda is," I said, trying to keep my lips in a straight line.

He groaned and pulled his pillow in to his lap. "I'm wearing unforgiving sweatpants and no underwear, as we've already established this fine morning."

"I'm flattered."

He palmed his face. "I'm horrified."

"Vincent, don't be embarrassed. I can't tell you how many boners I've gotten at the wrong time." Then I amended that. "Not that this is the wrong time. Hell, if you had more weight-lifting experience, I'd be making the most of it, lemme tell ya."

He dropped his hands and stared at me. Possibly more horrified than he was before. "That is not helping."

I chuckled. "Did you want me to leave the room for a few minutes, let you take care of it."

"No!"

"Want me to watch while you take care of it?"

"Oh my god!"

I laughed and put my hands up. "I'm just kidding. But now things aren't awkward."

"Not for you, maybe."

"One time in the eighth grade, I got a boner in history class. You know when you had to present your assignment in front of the whole class? It was a classic case of nervous boner, but until you've experienced that, then we can talk about awkward."

He laughed. "That can't have been good."

"Good? It was a great boner."

He burst out laughing. "That's not what I meant."

I grinned at him. "But you don't feel awkward anymore, right?"

He rolled his eyes and smiled. "Maybe."

"And I sneaked in a quick tutorial on how good hugs are and how boners don't need to be embarrassing. So as your tutor, I'm ahead of my schedule."

"So our next tutoring session together is strictly calculus?"

I made a face. "We might need to recap the kissing and hug section. Also not opposed to more boners."

He shot me a not-impressed eyebrow raise. "Exponential function, inverse functions, and logarithms it is then."

I sighed. "That sounds terrible. Painful, even."

He tossed his pillow toward the head of his bed. "I gotta go hit the showers."

I kept strict eye contact with him. "I'm trying really hard not to look at the boner sitch."

"Try harder."

"Then don't say the word harder."

"I . . . I have no more harder issue," he said, standing up and going to his drawers.

There was no boner but there was a decent outline.

Fuck.

"You said you wouldn't look!" he cried, holding his jeans in front of his crotch.

"I said I was trying not to. You're fucking sexy as hell, Vincent, and I'm a hot-blooded bisexual man. I'm sorry."

He rolled his eyes again.

I shrugged. "Would you like another hug?"

"No!"

"It was worth a shot."

He took his clothes and his toiletry kit. "Uh . . . Good luck in your game today."

"You'll be there, right?"

He nodded. "I shall be, yes. In the audience. If you want to look for me, I'll be the one there out of guilt and obligation, but there nonetheless."

I laughed. *So funny.* "I'll be the handsome one on the field with the 33 on my back."

He was smiling as he walked out, and I put my gear together and was smiling as I walked down to the Mundell house. It was the shared house I'd lived in the year before, where most of my friends still lived, and familiar smells and sounds hit me as I walked through the front door.

"Here he is," Ricky said as he hugged me. "Missed ya, big guy."

"I've seen you four days this week," I said.

"Yeah, but you don't live here anymore. How're the dorms treating ya? Terrible?"

"It's actually not so bad," I admitted.

He stopped and stared. "Not as cool as here though, right?"

I sniffed the air. "Well, the dorm smells better."

He laughed, because a house full of football players wasn't pretty, even on a good day. A lot of fun, but not pretty.

Jared walked in and gave me a fist bump. "Hey, Green! Thought you forgot where this place was."

"How could I forget that smell?" I scrunched my nose up. "Did Regan leave his socks near the air vent again?"

Jared laughed. "Probably. Now, Cobey, a little birdie told me a new guy was wearing your number at breakfast this morning."

I laughed but he was serious. "What?"

"Some guy you were lookin' all cozy with, laughing and what not."

Ricky slapped my shoulder. "You got yourself a new man, Cobes?"

Someone saw me and Vincent together at breakfast when he was wearing my number . . .

Oh man.

"Nah, that's just my roommate," I said, playing it down. "He was just wearing my hoodie because I made him. It's laundry day and I dragged him down to breakfast because I didn't want to sit by myself, and you know I gotta eat by nine on game day."

None of that was a lie.

The fact I made him join me because I also wanted to spend time with him was none of their business.

Jared gave me a smug smile. "They also said they saw you and the mystery guy having dinner this week too."

Okay, he needed to drop it. It was one thing to rib me about that shit, but Vincent wasn't out. Any rumors about me and him together could make things very bad for him.

"He's just my roommate. Nice guy. Doesn't smell. I mean, Christ, did this house always smell this bad?"

Ricky laughed. "If you came around more often, you'd be used to it again."

More guys filed into the kitchen and talk soon turned to the game. I was getting psyched for it, and by the time we got to the stadium, I was jumping.

I was also happy to not be thinking about Vincent. Not thinking about what he said about the library being the only safe place he had. Not thinking about him wearing my number. Not thinking about him getting a hard-on when we hugged. Not thinking about coming to watch me play today.

Yep.

Not thinking about Vincent at all.

# SIX

## VINCENT

I was no expert on estimating crowd sizes or how many seats the stadium held, but there must have been fifty thousand people there to watch the game.

A college football game.

Good lord. So many people.

How ridiculous.

But I found my seat and pretended to be engrossed by my phone as I sat by myself and the seats filled in around me. It was a home game, which meant the crowd looked like a sea of Franklin U's purple and gold.

I regretted not wearing anything in those colors, if for no other reason than to simply blend in. Not that I owned anything purple or gold, but still. I'd never considered myself to be the merch-wearing type. I'd never had the money to afford it.

"Who are ya rooting for?" the man beside me asked. He had a large soda in one hand, a plate of fries in the other, and an unfortunate mustache above a broad smile.

Oh god, he was speaking to me.

"Uh, Franklin," I replied, trying to smile. I considered, very briefly, telling him I didn't know much about football but thought better of it. Instead, I raised my fist. "FU Kings all the way."

I realized that was possibly the lamest thing I'd ever done, in a long list of lame things. The man was seemingly too excited to notice. "It's gonna be a good game. The Kings are a great team. Best college team in the state. Some names to keep an eye on, that's for sure. They'll be in the NFL soon, mark my words. Peyton Miller for sure. He'll be first pick of the draft next year."

I think I'd even heard of him, if that was any gauge of the guy's popularity. He was football royalty, apparently. His two dads had made huge waves being openly gay football players, and that was something that even my little closeted gay self knew.

"Ricky Rogers. He'll go the year after, I'd say."

I'd not heard of him.

"And Cobey Green. Linebacker. Only young but he's a big hitter. He'll go a long way."

*Well, I'd definitely heard of him. He kissed me last night and I rubbed my boner on his thigh this morning.*

That blunt thought aside, I hadn't expected a random stranger to talk to me about how good Cobey was. And that he was a big hitter. I couldn't imagine Cobey hitting anything.

Until the game started. I was stunned at seeing a whole lot of very fit looking guys wearing extremely tight pants. The uniforms were . . . god, I was going to say it. And my inner jock-hating prude was dying.

Because those uniforms were hot.

*And oh my god, there's number 33.*

It took me a second to get over the fact he was wearing pants *that* tight. Shiny gold tight pants that showed off his incredibly muscular legs, his thighs, and his ass.

Holy hell, his ass.

Even the purple jersey was tight around his waist and over his huge shoulder pads, and they made him look even bigger. He didn't need any help with that. He was huge already.

Then he was in the middle line behind the first line of guys that did the ball thing. And Cobey held his hand out, and I think he was yelling, though it was hard to hear over the noise of the crowd. The other team threw the ball back to some guy who looked to be about to throw it, but Cobey ran, flat out, lined up the guy with the ball, and literally smashed him over the line.

The crowd was on their feet, yelling, cheering, screaming.

The guys on the field all congratulated Cobey with slaps and knocks to his helmet.

I'd only just finished thinking that I couldn't imagine Cobey hitting anything, but apparently mowing them down was his thing.

Because he did it a lot.

He was fast and big and frighteningly good at demolishing his opponents.

And the uniform . . .

*Heaven help me, I think I'm becoming a fan of football.*

Well, I was a fan of football when Cobey was on the field. The other parts weren't nearly as exciting, even though the man beside me still hollered and whooped along with the rest of the stadium.

The mood was electric. It was exciting and contagious, and as much as I hated to admit it, I enjoyed it.

The Kings won, of course. And when the final horn went and the crowd's cheers died down and they all started to leave, I was left with a weird sense of . . . I wasn't sure. Melancholy?

The buzz was over, the adrenaline was gone, and I was going back to my dorm room to be by myself.

It just felt sad somehow.

Could I follow the crowd to Shenanigans? Sure.

Would I?

Absolutely not.

I had some schoolwork I could get done. It wasn't due for ages but there was no reason I couldn't get a head start on it. I'd have the room to myself for hours before Cobey came back. I could only guess that they'd be celebrating long into the night.

I was happy for him. Just a little sad for me, which was odd. I was more than used to being by myself. It wasn't too late. I could always go to the library instead . . .

And why had I told Cobey about the library? About how I would go there every day. About how my dad was never around much.

I'd never said that shit to anyone. No one.

Yet telling Cobey had been so easy.

So damn easy.

I grabbed a quick dinner from the dining hall, went up to my room, and began making notes for an assignment on how to interpret and apply principles underlying statistical data visualization, multivariate methods, and data mining.

Riveting stuff for a Saturday night.

I honestly wasn't expecting Cobey back until well after midnight, or even sometime the next morning, so I was surprised when the lock rattled just after eleven.

He came through the door, and seeing I was still awake, sitting against my headboard with a book in my lap, he grinned. "Hey," he said, dumping his gym bag at the foot of his bed. "I was trying to be quiet, but you're still up."

And then I noticed what he was wearing.

Suit pants and a button-down shirt. He hung the jacket up in his closet, giving me a nice view of his ass in those pants.

And I thought his football uniform was hot.

"Did you go somewhere fancy?" I asked. "What's with the suit?"

"Uh, no. Coach insists we be respectable after a game."

Okay, wow. I did not know that.

I didn't even want to guess where a guy Cobey's size went for a suit. Nothing off the rack, that was for sure.

*God, look at his thighs in those pants . . .*

*Stop staring, Vincent. Use words.*

"I, um, I didn't think you'd be back tonight," I admitted. I hated that I'd imagined him stumbling home at sunrise, half-dressed after doing god knows what with god knows whom. I hated that the idea of that made me feel nauseous. And I hated that him coming back early made me this happy.

"Ugh," he said, plonking himself on his bed and pulling his shoes and socks off. "The guys are partying on and I'm not twenty-one, so . . ."

This also surprised me.

"I thought you'd, you know, just party on with them anyway. You certainly could pass for twenty-one."

He began to unbutton his shirt. "Everyone knows I'm only nineteen. And if I got busted drinking, Coach would kill me. Then they'd need someone to bring me back to life so my parents could kill me."

Another button, and another button.

Holy shit.

*Don't look at his chest. Or at his fingers. Look up at his face, Vincent. Make eye contact.*

When I finally met his gaze, he was smiling at me. He knew damn well what he was doing. "So, did you watch the game?"

Um, game . . . game . . .

"Oh, yes. It was great," I said quickly. "Actually, I was surprised by how much fun it was."

This clearly made him happy. "Really?"

I nodded. "And I didn't know what was going on for any of it or what any of the rules are, but the atmosphere was fantastic. And I did notice the one guy, on the purple team, I think his number was 33? He smashed a lot of opponents."

Cobey grinned. "You saw that?"

"That? There were plural. Of course I saw you."

"And?"

"And what?" I said with a laugh. "You were great. I didn't

understand why you body slammed everyone, but every time you did, the crowd went crazy, so I assumed it was a good thing."

"Not a fan of the body slams?"

He was running out of buttons. I could see pecs and skin, holy shit . . .

*God, is it getting hot in here?*

*Stop staring at his body. His face, Vincent. Look at his face.*

It didn't help that his face was just as freaking gorgeous.

*And again with the words, Vincent. Use them.*

"I'm a fan of the uniform."

He laughed as he undid the last button, and he stood up so he could take it off. He had to almost peel it off, given the size of his arms. But he had huge pecs, defined abs, and those sexy-as-fuck V-muscles. A happy trail disappeared under the waistband, and he had red marks and welts over his arms, his ribs, and near his collarbone.

"Holy shit, Cobey, are you okay?"

I was up and off the bed, standing right in front of him before my brain had caught up.

But these were serious marks.

I almost touched the red line near his collarbone but stopped myself just short of contact. "Is this from football? Can I get you something?"

He didn't answer until I dragged my gaze up to his. Then he slowly shook his head. "I'm fine," he murmured. "Those body slams gotta leave a mark somewhere." His gaze went to my lips, then back to my eyes.

I realized then how close we were. That he was shirtless. That there seemed to be an electrical current in the room. I still had my hand raised as if to touch him, and I'd forgotten how to breathe again.

"You can touch me if you want," he said, his voice rough.

Holy fuck.

With a confidence I didn't know I had, I trailed my fingertip across the red mark near his collarbone. Maybe it was from his shoulder pads, I had no idea. But it was warm to the touch . . . I drew my finger slowly down his pec, watching a trail of goosebumps appear in its wake. His nipple was hard . . .

"Oh my god," I whispered.

"You like it?" he asked.

I nodded.

Then I used more fingers, the palm of my hand, and skimmed back up to his shoulder, down his biceps and up again, slowly down over his nipple to his abs.

His finger under my chin lifted my face, my mind was swimming, hazy, and he licked his lips.

He was going to kiss me, and I knew this time would be different.

His lips covered mine, soft and open, but there was intent in his touch. He kissed me, open-mouthed, and when his tongue touched mine, electricity shot through me and my knees almost buckled.

He pulled me close, wrapping his arms around me, and kissed me deeper, with his tongue and murmurs of pleasure that sent jolts of something divine through my bones.

I wanted more of whatever that was.

I clung to him, attempting to climb him like a tree. I wanted his tongue in my mouth and his hands all over my body. I wanted . . .

He broke the kiss and pushed me back to arm's length. He was breathless, he looked pained.

"Did I . . . did I do something wrong?" I asked. "I don't really know what I'm doing."

He laughed, though that looked painful too. "Ah, you did nothing wrong. At all. Actually, it was very right. I just need a minute because I'm about to skip a few weight-lifting tutorials, if you know what I mean."

I knew what he meant.

And I knew what I wanted.

I was wearing those thin sweatpants again. He could see how much I wanted it.

"Christ, you went commando again?" He put his hand to his forehead. "Vee, you're killing me."

My desire, my body, my dick far out ruled my bravado and rational thinking. I put my hand to his chest. "I don't want to stop."

## COBEY

Vincent looked me dead in the eyes, and if I thought there might be some fear or hesitation in his, there was none.

"I don't know how far I want to go, but I sure as hell don't want to stop now."

Oh god.

I slid my hand along his jaw and brought his forehead to mine. "If you want to stop at any time, you say stop, okay?"

He nodded. "Okay."

I kissed him again, sweeping my tongue to his. And I pulled him close, feeling his erection against my thigh. And he made a soft grunting sound that was like a match to kerosene.

I lowered him to his bed, my tongue still in his mouth, and pressed my full weight on top of him. He spread his legs and moaned.

Fuuuuuck.

I kissed down his jaw, down his neck, making his breath catch. He tilted his head and dragged his nails down my back.

My cock twitched and he gasped.

So fucking hot.

"Vincent," I said, just barely holding on. "Do you want to come?"

He froze, and I pulled back so I could see his face. There was a hint of uncertainty in his eyes, swirling with desire. He nodded.

"Say it."

"Yes," he whispered. "Please."

I crushed my lips to his, sucking his tongue into my mouth, his fingers digging into my back, my ass, my hair. He rocked his hips, his hard cock sliding against mine.

How was this his first time?

I leaned up on one hand and stroked him through his sweatpants. His eyes went wide and he groaned. He was far too close to draw this out, so I slipped my hand inside his pants and wrapped my fingers around his shaft. Hot, silky smooth, and rock hard.

"Fuck, Cobey."

His cockhead thrust in and out of my fist, smearing precome. He was so fucking hot underneath me. His body, lithe and receptive, and in that moment, completely at my mercy.

"You're gonna make me come," I said.

His cock pulsed in my hand. "Oh god," he rasped. He came in long spurts, his body jerking underneath me.

So fucking hot.

I undid the button on my suit pants, took out my cock. I was so turned on, so close, it just took a few quick pumps and I shot my load on his belly.

The room spun, and a dizzying high buzzed in my blood.

So good. *So fucking good.*

Vincent looked up at me, his lips kiss-swollen, his eyes full of wonder. "Holy shit," he whispered.

I laughed and collapsed on top of him, kissing him slow and lazy. "You okay?"

"I'm so much better than okay."

I chuckled, resting my head on my hand so I could stare at his face. His really beautiful face. "You're really hot, you know that?"

He blushed. "Uh . . ."

"And I'm having doubts that this was your first time fooling around because, holy fuck, that was so hot. You did everything right."

His blush deepened. "Oh, um, yes, definitely my first time."

I nudged my nose down his neck and licked and sucked the skin there.

He gasped. "And now, I, um, I see what the fuss is about."

"It's awesome, right?"

"Hell yes."

I sucked his earlobe into my mouth and he whined, his breaths short and sharp.

"I'd like to do more," he whispered. "A lot more."

I kissed up his jaw and claimed his mouth again, tasting his tongue.

God, was he getting hard again?

He rolled his hips, searching for the right kind of friction, and yeah. He was hard again. Or was it still? I wasn't sure.

But he explored more with his hands—my back, my shoulders, my hair. The perfect ratio of gentle and demanding, fingertips and nails. And he was more demanding with his lips and tongue when he kissed me.

I pulled back and he chased my mouth. I put my finger to his lips. "A question before we do anything else."

He nodded.

"Sexual health status," I said.

He frowned. "I'm a virgin," he mumbled. "You know that."

I lifted his chin so he had to look at me. "Hey. If I'm going to suck your dick, I have a right to know, okay?"

He stared. "You're going to . . ."

"I'd like to, if that's okay with you?"

He nodded quickly and licked his lips. "Um, yes. Of course, yes. God."

I peeled our stomachs apart from where our come had glued us together. It was a bit gross and kinda hot at the same time. But his erection was poking out the top of his sweatpants, and I couldn't wait to taste it.

I straddled his legs and pulled his pants down. His cock was long and thin with a pretty head that was begging for my mouth. I wrapped my hand around the base and looked up at his face. He was watching me intently, breathing hard.

"As a gay guy, you can't be embarrassed asking for a sexual health status. Ask for proof. Most guys have it on their phone these days. If they refuse or try to talk you down, then you walk away."

He nodded, and I realized that I could probably tell him anything right now—with my hand on his cock and the promise of my mouth—and he'd agree and nod. Which wasn't exactly fair.

"Vincent," I began.

"Sexual health status. Got it. Ask for proof. Walk away. Yep. Got it."

I smiled. "You sound a bit desperate," I said, slowly sliding my hand up his shaft.

He exhaled and let his head drop back. "I want . . . I want."

"You want me to do this?" I licked a line up the ridge of his cock. "And this?" I tongued the tip.

His head shot up, his expression desperation and desire. His chest rose and fell, his slim waist flexing tight. "Yes, Cobey, please."

Oh hell.

He used my name when he pleaded for it . . .

I took him into my mouth, warm and wet, licking and sucking while I pumped the base.

He nearly rose off the bed.

He tasted sweet and salty, and his quiet moans and gasps told me I was doing him just right. He watched me work him over, and I smiled around his cock.

"Oh fuck," he hissed. "I'm gonna come."

I sucked him harder, taking him deep. His swollen cock pulsed and twitched before emptying into my throat, and he cried out, his whole body tense.

I let him ride out the waves of his orgasm, knowing he

wouldn't be too coherent. I climbed off the bed, took a clean wash cloth, and poured some of my bottled water onto it. I wiped down my stomach, and then I kneeled over Vincent and wiped him down too.

He barely moved as I fixed his sweatpants, just wore a goofy smile and half-closed eyes. "You alive in there?" I asked.

"Mmm." His eyes focused on me and he grinned. "Fucking hell."

I laughed and climbed off his bed, stripped out of my clothes, and pulled on some briefs. I figured there was no point in hiding our bodies anymore. I pulled his bed cover over him, kissed his cheek, turned his reading light off, and climbed into my own bed.

I'd have liked to cuddle with him but didn't know if that would be weird.

"You okay over there?" I asked.

He replied with a sleepy laugh.

I waited for a few seconds to see if he was going to speak, but he didn't. Then I remembered I hadn't put my phone on the charger, so I got back up and pulled it out of my bag. I caught a glimpse of Vincent, sound asleep, still smiling.

He was so good-looking, even as he slept.

And the funny thing was, I'd kinda sworn off dating until I got my grades back on track, but I could see myself spending time with Vincent.

He was the opposite of anyone I'd ever been with, and I wasn't sure we had anything in common. But I'd be lying if I said I didn't like him.

Especially after today. First, breakfast and Vincent wearing my hoodie, then winning the game. And not just winning but me having the best game of my life. And then ending the day with orgasms.

It'd been the best day.

Kissing him had been incredible. Don't get me wrong. Having him under me, the hand job, watching him come, and of course the BJ. That was all hotter than hell.

But kissing him . . . when my tongue first touched his, I thought my heart might explode.

I could kiss him forever.

*Don't get ahead of yourself, Cobey.*

I lay back down in bed and sighed. It was all fine and well for my brain to tell me not to get ahead of myself, but I wasn't sure my heart was listening.

# SEVEN

## VINCENT

I WOKE up hungry which was something I hadn't done in a long time. Not since I moved to college, anyway. But my stomach woke me up, and I rolled over and saw Cobey still in bed, still asleep . . . and then I remembered.

Holy shit.

I'd had a night of three firsts.

My first French kiss. My first hand job, and my first oral sex experience.

I put my hand to my mouth to stop myself from laughing. It was ridiculous that I should feel this happy just because of physical gratification, but man . . .

"What's funny?" Cobey asked, his voice thick with sleep.

I sat bolt upright. "What?"

"You laughed."

"Out loud?"

He cracked one eye open. "Laugh in your head often?"

I chuckled. "Probably more often than out loud."

He squinted, then dug the heel of his hand into his eye socket. "So, what was funny?"

"Oh, nothing. Just . . . you know. Just that . . ."

"You had sex last night?"

"I didn't have sex."

"Orgasms with someone else is sex, Vee. It's all sex. Hand jobs, BJs." He scrubbed his hands over his face and sat up. The covers fell away to reveal his naked torso and his huge arms.

"The welts are still there," I said.

"Hm." He shrugged, unfazed. "Are you okay about last night? Everything that happened. No regrets?"

It was so like him to worry. "Zero regrets. The opposite of regrets, I think."

He grinned. "Good. Sometimes afterwards, reality kicks in. Especially when it's with a guy. I remember when I first hooked up with a girl, I was like 'heck yeah, chicks are hot,' and then after I hooked up with a guy the first time, it kinda rattled me. I mean, I was still like 'heck yeah, dudes are hot,' but it took a bit of mental gymnastics for me to realize it was okay."

"I think it validated something for me," I admitted. "That I am actually gay. It's one thing to be attracted to guys, but it's something else to act on it. But now I can say that yes, I'm very, very gay."

Cobey snorted out a laugh. "Well, I'm glad I could help with that. And it was my mom and dad who kinda helped me understand the bi thing. I mean, I knew what it was, of course. But that it was okay. And not just okay, that it was even a good thing."

"Your parents know?"

"Yeah, of course. Since I watched *The Avengers* when I was about twelve, and there was Black Widow and Hawkeye. Both equally hot." He shrugged. "And Iron Man, and Thor, and Loki because damn. Actually, that whole movie was confusing for me, and I guess I asked too many questions, and my mom said it was okay."

My god, he was so cute.

"Does your dad know?" he asked.

"That the cast of *The Avengers* are all equally hot? I'm not sure."

He laughed. "No. That you're gay."

My heart sank and I shook my head. "Oh no. Nope. We aren't close. At all. He . . . he, uh, he never . . ." Shit. Just stop talking, Vincent. "We aren't close."

Cobey studied my face for a few seconds. "I'm sorry."

"Me too."

"Got brothers or sisters?"

"Nope. You?"

He shook his head. "Nah. It's just me." He scratched his head and threw the covers back so he could put his feet on the floor. He let out a groan as he moved.

"Are you sore?"

He nodded. "A bit. Feel like I ran a few miles while repeatedly smashing other guys into the ground."

I smiled. "Does it help to know you looked amazing while doing that?"

He laughed. "It does help, yes."

"Those tight pants, and the jersey. Actually the whole outfit is top tier."

"Outfit?"

"Uniform." I shrugged. "Same thing."

He laughed again and stood up slowly, stretching out his back with a groan.

In his underwear.

With morning wood.

And a body like Adonis.

Sweet mercy, all hail the god of beauty and attraction.

Right in front of my face.

"Wow."

"See something you like?"

I looked up at his face. It took some effort to look away from the giant cock snug in his briefs, but I did it. He was smirking. "Um, yes," I admitted. "I like it very much, apparently."

His grin widened and his tongue peeked out from the corner of his mouth. He looked as if he was considering something but then changed his mind. He shook his head, pulled on some shorts. "I'm very tempted to give you more tutorials right now, but I don't think that's a good idea."

"Why not?"

"Because . . ."

I shrugged. "I'm a quick learner."

He dropped his hands and let his head fall back. "You're not making it easy."

"What kind of lesson? Just out of curiosity."

"The art of sucking dick."

Holy shit. "Oh." I blinked a few times. "Well, if it's an art, then it does imply that practice should be applied."

He sighed and picked up his toiletry kit. "I need a shower and breakfast. How about you?"

I looked at his dick. "Uh, yeah, I could eat."

"Fucking hell, Vincent," he breathed. He dropped his toiletry kit onto his bed and let out a slow, measured exhale.

He was so close to giving in. The bulge in his shorts was impressive, and I wanted it.

I licked my lips. "I can't promise I'll be any good at it. You're kinda big."

He turned quickly and stood in front of me where I sat on my bed. "Open your mouth," he said, sliding his shorts down and pulling out his erection.

He was big. So much bigger now that it was shoved in my face.

"Flatten your tongue," he said, his voice gruff.

I did as he instructed, and with his fist around the base, he tapped the head onto my tongue.

"Lick it," he murmured. "Underneath, lick the head. Tongue the slit and taste me."

Holy.

Fucking.

Shit.

I did what he said, tasting his salty precome.

He let out a shaky breath. "Use your hands," he whispered. "Pump me, stroke me. Cup my balls."

He was going to make *me* come at this rate. But I did what he asked, and I must have done it right because he moaned and his cock twitched.

"Open wide," he murmured.

I did. And I wanted this so bad. I was so aroused, like he was sucking me off and not the other way around.

I took him into my mouth, my lips closing around him.

"Just take the tip," he said, his voice tight.

I sucked the head into my mouth and tried to use my tongue at the same time. He made a strangled sound, so I looked up to find him looking down at me.

"Fuck, you're so hot," he said. His cock swelled, hardened in my mouth, and he pulled out. His hand covered mine, pumping hard, and shot his load onto my chest.

Watching his cock spill right in front of me, onto me, was so hot. I was so close to coming and I hadn't even touched my own dick.

I shoved my hand down my sweatpants, but Cobey stopped me. "Let me," he said, pushing me until I was lying back, my feet still on the floor, his hand on my cock.

He leaned over me, his face above mine, and he jerked me off, staring into my eyes as I came. Pleasure burned in every cell of my body, my mind was gone, and the room spun.

Cobey looked down at me and laughed. "You okay?"

I had to catch my breath and swallow, trying to think coherent thoughts. My answer came out as a snort, and Cobey laughed again. He pulled me up to sit, then lifted my T-shirt over my head. "You can't be wearing jizz shirts anywhere."

Jizz shirts.

I laughed again and he lifted my eyelid and peered in. "Are you in there?"

I batted his hand away. "I think I experienced a structural integrity malfunction. You know what? I need to apologize to Mr. Shelton."

"Who?"

"Mr. Shelton. My science teacher in my freshman year of high school. I need to tell him you can have both a chemical and physical changes at a molecular level in a living thing, and that chemical change could be reversible under the correct conditions."

Cobey laughed again. "What are you talking about?"

"My bones are jelly."

He pulled me to my feet and hugged me. "You are the funniest guy I know."

I would have argued that point, but he was still hugging me and it felt amazing. It was warm and safe, and my god . . . Was human touch always this good?

"Do you feel okay about what we did?" he asked.

I nodded against his bare chest. So warm and perfect. "Yeah."

"So about that shower and breakfast idea . . ."

"Yes, I'm starving."

He looked around and went to grab his hoodie off the end of his bed but stopped short. Then his eyes shot to mine and he made a face. "Um, I was going to give you this, but about that . . . yesterday, one of the guys said someone saw us at breakfast with you wearing my hoodie with my number. They wanted to know who you were, of course. I just said you were my roommate and it was laundry day and you needed something to wear, which sounds kinda lame now that I think about it. But I panicked because you're not *out* and I didn't want anyone to assume you were because it might have looked that way . . . given you were wearing my number while you were with me, and they all know I'm bi, so they probably just assumed you were . . . well, not straight. I'm sorry."

Shit.

"It's okay," I said. "I don't care what other people think. It's not like I know a lot of people. And let's be real, it's not like they'd think you'd be with someone like me."

He frowned. "What's that supposed to mean?"

"Uh, hello? Mr. Popularity King." I gestured to him, and then to me. "And Mr. Nobody."

"You're not nobody," he said seriously. "And I don't appreciate you assuming I would care about someone's social status if I wanted to date them or not. I'm pretty sure we've had this conversation before, and I said we needed to work on the way you see yourself because, Vincent, I've done my fair share of sex stuff with other people and I'm telling you, you're the hottest person I've ever been with. So . . ." He snatched up his hoodie, and while I was too stunned to speak, he shoved my head through the head hole, then pulled each of my arms through like he was dressing a toddler. "How about you wear the hoodie and let people think whatever the fuck they want to think because you are *exactly* the type of guy I would be with. And maybe if people weren't such assholes, they might realize that the not-popular people are still people too."

Right, then.

Okay.

He grinned. "You good?"

"Um. I think so?" I wasn't exactly sure, but . . . "It's kinda hard to be mad or embarrassed that you just dressed me as if I was a toddler when you say awesome stuff like that."

He picked up his toiletry kit and slung his towel over his shoulder. "People not treating others like people is a pet peeve of mine."

"I can tell."

He grabbed my toiletry kit and pressed it to my chest. "And I meant what I said about you being sexy as fuck. You totally have a sultry twink vibe going on that presses buttons I didn't know needed pressing." Then he took my towel and threw it over my shoulder. "Now please, shower and then breakfast because I need food."

I wore his hoodie to the showers but I didn't wear it to break-fast. He saw it neatly folded on the end of his bed but didn't say anything. I was already dressed in my jeans and a T-shirt, pulling on my Converse when he came back from the showers. He was just wearing shorts, and when he pulled a shirt over his head, I saw another red welt on his back.

"Does it hurt getting hit when you play football?" I asked.

"Sometimes, but we're padded up pretty well. Most of these welts are from the pads, like the edging or whatever when we get hit. But it's not so bad." He lifted one leg to show me his calf. There were red lines, already bruising. "Cleats hurt, but only afterwards. I don't feel it on the field."

The mark on his forearm was bruising up as well.

"Have you considered a sport with less contact?"

He laughed. "And where would the fun in that be?" He shuf-fled into his slides and went to the door. "Come on. I need fooooooood."

I was beginning to think that was a reoccurring theme with him.

He loaded his plate with a mountain of food while I stuck to toast and coffee, but I added an extra slice and some diced fruit for Cobey.

Almost every single person we encountered congratulated him on an awesome game. Some gave me a second look. Some even smiled. But he didn't choose to sit with them, and he never left to chat with someone, not even for a second. He sat with me, and it was hard not to feel a bit special, even if we couldn't exactly talk much because of the constant interruptions.

"What're your plans for today?" he asked.

"You say plans as though implying I have a social life."

He laughed as he bit into his toast, but he still waited for my answer.

So, I sipped my coffee and laid out just how much of a loser I was. "Laundry, which is riveting stuff. Then schoolwork. Which is even more riveting."

"You don't go down to the beach or the pier?"

I cringed. "You mean outside?"

He chuckled. "I gotta go catch up with the guys this morning. It's a team thing. But maybe this afternoon we could go to the beach."

"To swim? In the ocean? Where there are sharks?"

He smiled as he sipped his juice. "Or maybe we could take a ball and you can show me how you throw."

Oh good lord, no. "I'd rather take my chances with a great white shark than let you see me throw a ball."

He laughed again, louder this time. People around us stopped and looked.

I shoved the bowl of fruit over to him. "Or we could take your calculus books and get some of my tutorials done."

His eyes widened, his smile died. "I thought you were my friend."

I snorted. "It was part of our deal, remember? Actually, I think we're behind on your calculus lessons. We've done three of your tutorials and none of mine. You're losing out here."

He leaned in and whispered, "I don't think either of us are losing from my tutorials."

I tried really hard not to blush. "Is taking your books to study outside not helping me socialize? Is having breakfast with you not me being out in public?"

"I guess. Though my indoor tutorials are much more fun."

"Which is why we should probably do my tutorials outside, because if we do them in our room, they're likely to become your tutorials. If you know what I mean."

He grinned and did some subtle eyebrow thing. "Oh, I know what you mean. I have the mental imagery burned into my brain of you this morning—"

"Hey, Green," a guy said as he walked over.

I coughed and sat up straight.

Fuck.

Cobey turned to the guy. "Hey, Gavin. Wassup?"

"Just checking to see if your leg was okay."

"My leg?"

"Yeah. From kicking ass all day long yesterday."

Cobey laughed and nodded. "Yep. Leg's fine. Ready to do it all again this weekend."

Gavin offered Cobey his fist for a bump, then he looked at me. And waited.

"Oh," Cobey said. "Gavin, this is Vincent, Vincent, Gavin. He's on the wrestling team."

Cobey offered no information on me, and from the look on Gavin's face, I got the impression that was what he was really after. He wore a Franklin U wrestling shirt, and a fake smile. I also got the impression Cobey didn't like him too much, which was a first. He seemed to like everyone, but not this guy.

I had no idea we even had a wrestling team. I also tried to not let the fact Cobey didn't seem to like him sway my opinion. "Nice to meet you," I said, trying to act braver than I felt.

He nodded once. "Hey." But then he kept staring at me as if he wanted me to continue the conversation.

Cobey finished his juice and stood up with his tray. "Good to see you, man. But I gotta get going. Got the after-game meet with the guys. You know how it is. But we'll catch you around, probably at Shenanigans sometime, yeah?"

"Yeah, sure," Gavin said, hopes of more conversation now gone.

Cobey was really good at giving people the nicest brush-off.

We cleared off our trays—I could feel people watching us—and then on the way back to our room, another three people congratulated Cobey on his game. It was mind boggling to me but he took it all in stride. Or more to the point, he thrived on it.

I found it all a bit exhausting.

As soon as we got back into our room and the door was closed, I flopped down on my bed.

"You okay?" Cobey asked.

"I don't know how you do it."

"Do what?"

"Talk to people all the time."

He laughed and sprayed some more deodorant under his arms. "I gotta get going. You've got until about four o'clock to prepare for your next social outing."

I sighed. "You mean to prepare for your next calculus lesson."

He grimaced. "Ouch."

I was still smiling after he'd left, the smell of his deodorant in the air, the memory of what we'd done this morning fresh in my mind. The sight of him, the taste of him, the feel of his cock in my mouth.

My dick certainly liked that memory. I gave myself a squeeze and groaned out a laugh.

How was this my life?

How did I, Vincent Brandt, find myself fooling around with Cobey Green?

Now that I'd woken up my sex drive, I never wanted it to end. I wanted to live in the feel of physical touch, of sensation and anticipation, of orgasms.

I just had to find a way to ignore the feeling of butterflies and excitement. I had to ignore the way he looked at me, his smile . . . After all, he was nice to everyone, he chatted and laughed with *everyone*. It didn't make me special.

And with that brutal reminder, I rolled over and grabbed my stats textbook, opened to algorithm design, and began to read.

THE SOUND of the lock on the door startled me. I was even more startled to see Cobey come in, his usual grin in place. I checked the time on my phone. It was 3:45 p.m.

Oh.

"Let me guess," he said. "You lost track of time."

I closed my books. "Uh, yes."

"Did you eat lunch?"

"Um . . ."

He clucked his tongue and nodded toward the door. "Come on."

I got to my feet, mostly out of panic. "Where are we going?"

"Down to the pier."

I looked at what I was wearing. "I'm not—"

"You look fine," he said.

That was hardly the truth but I had little option. It wasn't like I had much else to choose from in my wardrobe. Going down to the dining hall was one thing, but heading out in public with Cobey Green, wearing my old, no-name-brand clothes made me feel insecure.

I hated that feeling.

"Are you worried about being cold?" he asked, so sincerely it made my heart squeeze. "It's warm in the sun but you can bring a jacket if you want."

He honestly didn't care about my clothes. Hell, he didn't even notice. It made me like him even more.

"I'm sure I'll be fine," I replied. "Just don't forget your calculus book."

"You're really going to make me do that?"

"Yep. Exams will be here before you know it."

He sighed and sagged, looking like I'd stolen his favorite candy bar. But he grabbed his book and off we went, heading out through the quad, across the street and toward the pier.

There were a lot of people around for a Sunday. Walking dogs, jogging, pushing strollers, sitting on the sand. There was even a game of volleyball happening farther up the beach.

It was actually a pleasant day. If the sun, sand, surf, and social-izing was your thing.

We walked to the pier and he went straight to a taco stand. "You need to eat."

I shook my head. "I, uh, I don't have the money," I whispered. "Sorry, if I'd known . . ."

He gave my arm a squeeze and ordered anyway. Enough to feed a family of four, apparently, including two sodas, and cheerfully handed me his textbook so he could pay and carry the food. We found a seat and he handed me a container that had two tacos in it.

"Thank you," I said quietly.

"It's no problem." He bit into one of his many tacos and spoke with his mouth half-full, still somehow managing to look cute. "I eat enough for two. You eat like a bird." He sipped his drink and shrugged. "My parents give me a card for food and whatever. They know I eat a lot, and my mom swears it's cheaper than having me at home. I can rack up a grocery bill, don't you worry."

I chuckled. "I've seen you eat."

He finished his first taco. "I know I'm lucky. It's a privilege to have folks that can do that for me. It'd be hard for me to find casual work with my training schedule, and I'm supposed to be concentrating on my studies." He rolled his eyes. "We both know how well that's going."

I knew it was my turn to share something about me, and if I wanted him to know about my situation, then now was my chance. I didn't like talking about this stuff but I trusted Cobey, and maybe it would help him understand my position at Franklin U.

So I took a deep breath, looked out across the ocean, and talked.

## COBEY

"My mom bailed when I was four," Vincent said. "My dad didn't really want to be a single parent, or a parent at all, really. I mean, he did okay. He just wasn't around much. Or at all, sometimes. He worked away a lot, so I spent most nights in our house alone, even as young as four. I grew up in Millside. I don't know if you've heard of it."

I nodded, my voice quiet. "I've heard of it."

Most people had. Just saying that explained a lot. Low income, low employment, high crime, empty businesses, welfare housing.

I couldn't even imagine a four-year-old kid being all alone at night.

"We didn't have much," he said. "Dad kept the electric bill paid, so that was good. But there was never much food in the house. I'd live on sandwiches for days at a time because it was all I knew how to make. It was all we had in the cupboard. Peanut butter and jelly."

"Jesus, Vincent, I'm sorry."

He smiled out to sea. "One good thing my dad did was put me in school early. He just did it so I'd be looked after during the day, but school became my safe haven. I was smart, avoided trouble by avoiding everyone and hanging out in the school library."

"And you went to the public library after school," I added. He'd said that before; I was just connecting the dots.

His eyes met mine and he nodded. "And on weekends, and school breaks. I must have read every book in that place. Every single one. From preschool to senior year."

Man, that nearly broke my heart. From preschool . . . He was just a baby looking out for himself. I wanted to hug him, and hold him, but I couldn't do that out in public so I settled on giving his arm a gentle squeeze.

"The ladies in the library were so nice to me, and Mrs. Collingwood kept me busy with extra worksheets she'd print off for me. She said I was gifted and my brain was like a sponge and I needed to water it with information."

"That's really sweet."

He nodded, smiling. "She was great. And old Mrs. Camp next door. She'd keep an eye out for me, feed me every once in a while. But she didn't have much either. Authorities came around once, on a day when my dad was actually in town. Not that they cared much."

Christ.

"Anyway, as I got older, my dad told me to leave school and get a job, help bring some money in, or maybe just not be a drain on him anymore. I don't know."

Fucking hell. Imagine calling your kid a financial drain.

"When I told him I was applying for colleges, he told me I was on my own. Not that I expected him to be able to help at all. I got a few offers from all over, but Franklin was a full scholarship. I couldn't say no to that. I still have to cover part of the dorm fees, which is why I do tutoring, and I can budget for it but it's pretty tight."

"You know what?" I said. "I think you're pretty awesome."

He laughed, his cheeks tinged pink. "Yeah, not really."

"Yes, really."

He sighed and took a small bite of his taco. "You asked me before what I wanted to do when I was done with college, and I said data scientist because of the money."

I nodded.

"I don't want obscene amounts or to be super rich. I just want *enough*. And I'd like to think that money isn't a motivating factor, but when you don't have enough to buy food or clothes, and you can't go on school field trips or play sports because you don't have enough, then yeah, it's a motivating factor."

"I suppose it would be, yeah." I wasn't sure what else I could say.

He was quiet for a bit. Then he held up his remaining taco. "I appreciate this though. It's so good. I mean, the food in the dining hall is okay, but this is . . . it's amazing."

"Tacos are awesome, and that mac'n'cheese the other day was an abomination. Promise me that whenever that shit is on the menu, you'll let me buy you some tacos and we will come down here to eat them."

He chuckled. "Maybe." He finished his taco, wiped his hands, and sipped his drink. "Sorry to be a downer. I didn't mean to dump all that on you."

I knocked my knee to his. "Don't be sorry. I'm glad you told me. You know, Vee, I have mad respect for you. I know damn well I've had it easy. I've never had to worry about not having food to eat or the right gear for all the football camps and training shit I've done. I'm privileged as fuck, and I know it."

"But you don't flaunt it," he offered. "You're nice to everyone. It doesn't matter what they wear or what group they're in. At first I just thought you were super popular because you're some big football star, but honestly, it's because you treat everyone the same." I met his gaze, and he blushed and smiled at the ocean. "Don't look at me like that. It's true."

"Look at you like what?"

"Like you want . . . like . . . you know what I mean."

"Like I want to kiss you right now?"

The red bloomed down his neck under his shirt, and so god help me, I wanted to lick it.

"If we were in our room right now," I teased, "I'd be all over you."

He laughed, shocked and embarrassed. "Which is why I suggested we bring this out here," he said, shoving my textbook at me. "Otherwise we'd never get anything done, and I've never failed a tutorial yet."

I took my book and realized that I really needed to do this. He was kind enough to offer his time, and after hearing about how hard he fought to be here, it made me want to try harder too.

I wasn't kidding when I said I'd had it easy. I didn't know what it meant to struggle like he did, so the very least I could do was take his time seriously.

I flipped open the book to chapter two.

# EIGHT

## VINCENT

THE NEXT TWO weeks were awesome, some of the happiest times of my life, and confusing if I was being honest.

Cobey and I settled into some kind of routine of breakfast together, classes during the day, tutoring for me of an afternoon, training for him, sometimes even dinner together. Oh, and a lot of making out in our room.

It usually ended with mutual orgasms, which was fine by me, but it was mostly exploring bodies and a lot of kissing.

And I gotta say . . . his body was a work of art to explore. I was way more confident in that area too. But it wasn't all about me.

We also managed to get through some calculus. He was trying really hard to understand it and I could see it wasn't easy for him, but he was trying. He got frustrated with it, which I could understand, and I really hated that he got a bit down on himself too.

But he hadn't given up yet.

As for my tutorials, as if the breakfast and dinner experiences weren't bad enough, he'd insisted I go to the coffee shop with him, *twice*. Last weekend he'd had an away game so I hadn't gotten to watch him play, but I heard all about it from the whole school, basically.

"Good game, Green!"

"Awesome play, man!"

"You really kicked some ass!"

The passing comments and high fives didn't stop, but at least people had stopped staring at me. Mostly. I figured they'd lost interest in why Cobey was spending so much time with me when they'd heard we were roommates.

But people smiled at me more, in the corridors or in class. I tried to smile back, simply because I didn't want them to think less of Cobey. And over the course of the two weeks, it got easier.

I even said hi a few times.

I wasn't sure if this was part of his *socialization* plan, but I was meeting new people. Kind of. In passing. If *meeting* meant awkwardly smiling at from a distance.

Still, it was more socializing than I'd done in well, forever.

And my friends were starting to notice. And when I say friends, I mean Rafe.

It was a Friday afternoon, classes were done, and I walked into the library to wait for my first session, like I always did. Early, like I always was.

"Hey, Vincent," he said cheerfully.

"Hi. How's your day been?"

"Good, good," he said, walking around the table with two binders in his hands. He looked at me, stopped, sighed, and put the binders down. "Okay, spill the deets."

I held onto my backpack tight, as if it could possibly shield me. "Deets on what?"

He stepped in close and sat on the table right next to me. "What's going on with you?"

I instinctively fixed my hair and took my glasses off to check them. "What do you mean?" My shirt was clean. I'd just done laundry . . .

He smiled and shook his head. "No, you look fine. I mean,

what's going on with you? These last few weeks, you've been . . . I dunno. Like you know the world's best kept secret."

I swallowed hard. "That's not true."

He gave me a smug nod. "You've been joined at the hip with a certain football player. And I've said absolutely nothing, I promise you. But people are starting to talk."

"Talk? About what?"

"That Cobey Green is off the market."

"He's what?"

"Off the market. As in, no longer single." He raised an eyebrow at me. "Know anything about that?"

Shit. Shit, shit. "No. Why would I? We're not . . . I mean, he's not . . ."

He dropped his voice. "Vincent."

"We . . . Goddammit, Rafe." I put my hand to my forehead and sighed. *Fucking hell.* "I don't know if you know this, but you're the only person on campus who knows that I'm . . ." I looked around to double-check we were alone. We were, but I still whispered the next part. "Gay."

He stared.

"Not that I told you directly, I realize. But I hinted by omission. Actually, you're not the only one because Cobey knows. So that makes two of you. Not that I tell people I'm *not* gay. It's more the point that I don't talk to other people. So it's not exactly public knowledge."

"Hey," he said gently. "It's okay. You don't have to tell people anything. But I'm going to say this, and I don't want you to freak out." He put his hand on my arm. "I think people might have assumed you are. I mean, if they're assuming you and Cobey are together, then that makes you gay, or bi, or something that's not strictly het. Know what I mean?"

I tried not to panic but there was a bubble of anxiety and dread rising in my body, from my feet up to my belly and my chest—

He squeezed my arm. "It's totally cool, Vincent. It's one

hundred percent cool. Franklin has a huge LGBTQ family. Pretty sure there's more queer people here than straight."

"That's statistically improbable and factually highly unlikely," I said, but he smiled and I understood then that he was just trying to defuse the panic bomb. It worked. I sighed and let my head fall back. "God, I don't even know why I care."

"Because it's often a secret kept for self-preservation," he said.

That was so freaking true.

"Just remember," he added, "you don't need to confirm anything or tell anyone any damn thing that's not their business."

I nodded. "Yeah, thanks."

"You okay?" he asked gently.

"Yeah, sure."

"Good." He looked past my shoulder. "Because you've got company."

I turned around to find Cobey walking in, still in his sweaty practice gear, grinning from ear to ear. My heart skipped several beats and my stomach swooped. Rafe clapped me on the arm and walked away.

"Sorry to interrupt," Cobey said. "Everything okay?"

"Yeah," I said, even though the jury was still out. "What are you doing here?"

He was holding a slip of paper, which he gave to me. "Ticket for the game tomorrow. You gotta come watch me play. I just got it, and the team's heading down to Shenanigans. I thought I'd drop it in for ya on my way. Before I lose it."

"Oh, thank you."

"I won't be late tonight. Gotta play tomorrow. Unless you wanted to come down to the bar when you're done here?"

Walk, by myself, into a crowded college bar full of football players and half the student body? Cobey would be the only person I'd know and he'd have to speak to me and people would definitely stare and then the rumor mill would be on fire. "You know what? I really don't want to do that. But thanks for asking."

"Another day, maybe."

"When there's no people there, sure."

He laughed. "I gotta get going or the guys'll come looking for me."

"Okay. See you later."

"Yes, you will."

He left with the same smile he arrived with, and it must have been contagious because my traitorous face was doing something similar as I watched him leave. I turned around to find Rafe watching me.

He walked over, chewing on the inside of his lip. "Dude, it's no wonder people are saying he's off the market. Is that how you two are around each other all the time?"

My insides felt like jittery goo. "How are we around each other? We were just talking. He gets a ticket for me to watch his game." I held it up as proof. "That's all."

"Vincent, my man, this is gonna come as a shock to you, but that guy . . ." he said, thumbing the direction Cobey just left. "That huge as fuck, handsome as hell guy, is in love with you."

In.

Love.

. . .

What the . . . ?

"Don't be ridiculous," I said, rolling my eyes. "That's the most absurd thing I've ever heard."

Rafe pointed to his eyes. "He had hearts in his eyes when he was talking to you just now. Literal hearts. I thought that shit only happened in cartoons."

"He did not."

"He looked like an anime character."

"Rafe . . ."

"Vincent."

"Don't be absurd."

He shook his head. "I'm telling you. As a friend. That man has it bad for you."

I shook my head, dismissing that entire notion, because no. It was ludicrous.

Wasn't it?

"You two are . . . spending time together, right?"

The way my face burst into flames answered that question.

"And you share a room, so I'm guessing it's pretty frequent."

Was spontaneous combustion possible? It sure felt like it. I looked around for the fire extinguisher.

"I'll take that as a yes. Lucky for some," he murmured.

This was horrifying.

"Is he seeing anyone else?" Rafe asked.

Oof. That thought hit me hard. "What? Uh, no? I don't think so." He didn't have time. He went to class and he practiced, and he spent time with me, that was it.

"He's not hooking up at the bar right now, is he?"

My brain fritzed and it took me a second to think. "Why would you say that? Why would you even put that in my head?"

Rafe put both his hands on my shoulders. "Vincent, I'm telling you he's not hooking up with anyone because he has hearts in his eyes for you. And your reaction right now told me you feel the same."

I blinked. "Wh-what?"

He sighed with a smile. "I'm just helping you out. Like I'd help someone with a literary assessment on understanding characters by their actions and reactions alone. His actions and your reaction, it's a textbook character analogy."

"Feels more like a character assassination."

Rafe snorted and raised both hands. "I'll say no more. But if you didn't know before, now you do. To be honest, I don't know how you didn't realize what you're feeling because, dude, since when do you go to football games?"

I looked at the ticket in my hand. Maybe Rafe had a point . . . I shrugged. "He's really good and he wears those tight pants and the tight-fitting shirts that show off everything, and I mean, I've seen him naked plenty—"

Rafe cleared his throat and nudged me with his elbow. "Hi, Amber," he said, welcoming my first tutorial session.

She waved and went to our usual table. "Just be a minute," I said, trying not to die.

*God, that was close.*

Rafe tried not to laugh but barely succeeded. "I'd say have a good weekend but that's probably a given, so instead I'll say don't overthink it, don't over-analyze it. And don't worry about the gossip or the haters. They're just jealous because they want what you're getting." He winked and left me to die of mortification on my own.

I somehow managed to get through my two tutoring sessions without being totally useless but by the time I got back to my room, what Rafe had said to me was all I could think about.

*That guy is in love with you.*

*Is he at the bar hooking up with someone?*

*He had hearts in his eyes.*

*Like an anime character.*

*Your reaction tells me you feel the same.*

*Is he hooking up with someone?*

Sitting on my bed, I had no hope of eating food, my stomach was in knots. How could Rafe tell me Cobey was in love with me and then ask me if he was hooking up with other people?

I had no experience with this.

Zero.

I wouldn't have thought Cobey would be the type to cheat, but there were a few problems with this. One, we weren't technically together. Two, we'd never discussed any such parameters. And given we weren't technically together, no such parameters should need discussing. Three, we'd never even discussed what we'd expect from any relationship, ours or others, and I had no idea what Cobey wanted.

Maybe he wanted to hook up with whomever he wanted. He surely didn't have a lack of admirers. Maybe he was hooking up with someone right now? Maybe he was—

The sound of keys in the door startled me.

Maybe he was coming back now? Oh god, if he had someone with him and wanted me to leave . . .

The door opened and Cobey came in. Alone. Smiling. "Hey," he said, bright as ever.

"Oh, hey," I replied.

He studied me for a second and closed the door. "Everything okay?"

"Oh sure," I lied. "Yeah, why wouldn't it be?"

His eyebrows furrowed for a second as if he could tell I was lying. He came and sat on my bed. "So there's something I need to tell you," he said gently.

*Oh god.*

*Here we go.*

"Do you have someone waiting in the hall and need me to disappear for a while?"

His eyes went wide. "What? No, oh my god." Then he laughed. "You're so funny."

Except I wasn't trying to be. "Okay then. Um, what did you want to tell me?"

"Some of the guys were ribbing me tonight, you know, the usual football banter."

I didn't know, but I could guess.

"Anyway, it was all meant to be harmless, but apparently people around college have been talking, and there were some photos . . ."

"Photos of what?"

"Of us."

The blood whooshed from my head to my feet. "Us doing what?" I looked around our room. "How?"

He seemed confused, then he realized what I meant. "Oh no, no, not photos of us doing anything in here, my god."

I clutched my heart. "Jesus."

He took my hand. "I'm sorry. I didn't mean to scare you like that."

My heart was still hammering. "Well, photos of us anywhere else can't be that bad, can they?"

He shook his head. "No, they're not bad. They're just . . . well, people are talking . . ." He sighed, then just blurted it all out. "People think we're a thing. There are a lot of rumors on social media, apparently, and you know I don't give a shit what people say about me, but they're just assuming you're gay, or bi, or I dunno. Not straight."

Relief flooded through me. "Oh, yeah, Rafe told me about it this afternoon."

"So you know? What people are saying?"

I shrugged. "Well, not exactly. No one's said anything to my face, so . . ."

"But Vincent, you're not out. These rumors are basically gonna force you out of the closet, and that's not fair."

"Maybe it's doing me a favor?" I shrugged with a sigh. "Now I don't have to tell anyone. It's not like I speak to people, and I told Rafe already, so that's okay."

"What about your dad?"

I shook my head. "He's not exactly a big part of my life. Or a part of any kind, to be honest. I'm not much use to him. And when I said I was going to college, that kind of sealed the deal."

"Fucking hell, Vee." He frowned and held my hand. "I'm so sorry."

"Don't be sorry. I'm in college. It's all I ever wanted." I tried to smile with a courage I didn't exactly feel. "And maybe part of my college life is getting to be the real me. Gay and not hiding that part of me."

He smiled proudly and squeezed my hand.

"I'm not saying I'll be making any huge announcements, because being the center of attention for any reason is horrifying. But if people want to think I'm gay, then let them. I'm not ashamed."

He leaned in and kissed my cheek. "You're kinda great, you know that?"

No, but anyway. "You said there were photos?"

"Oh." He took out his phone and went to what I think was the FU student Discord threads. He scrolled for a second then turned his phone around to show me. It was a photo of us in the dining hall. We were sitting by ourselves, like we normally were, and whoever took the photo was behind me, a few tables away. "There's just a few photos and they're all pretty much the same."

In the photo, it appeared that I was talking and Cobey was smiling or laughing, looking at me like I hung the moon.

*He has hearts in his eyes. Like an anime character.*

Oh.

And the caption read *Find someone who looks at you like Cobey Green looks at Vincent Brandt.*

Oh my god. "They know my name?"

Cobey chuckled and threaded our fingers. "People know who you are because of me. They've seen us talking and they had to find out. I'm sorry. I know you must hate that."

I wasn't sure what to feel. This whole day had been a bit of a ride. "I'm certainly not used to people knowing who I am. Or caring. I've noticed people smiling at me more. Some even spoke to me."

He smiled at that. "How did that go?"

"I panicked the first time."

Now he laughed, and he leaned in and kissed me, soft and sweet. "Are you okay?"

I nodded. "Yeah. I am now."

"Did you really think I'd have someone in the hallway and would ask you to bail for a bit?"

"I've had a very weird afternoon," I said, then wishing I hadn't because I didn't want to explain my entire mental break-down. "Just with what Rafe said, and random people talking to me in the corridors and stuff."

"Do you need a cuddle? Maybe some making out?"

I rolled my eyes, but my smile was answer enough. He jumped up, grabbed my ankle, and pulled me down the bed.

Then he laid himself down, somehow scooping me into his arms with my head on his chest, and our legs entwined.

"Better?"

I looked up at him and this time I kissed him. "Much."

## COBEY

I played awesome. Maybe not as well as my last home game but better than last week, and I was starting to think maybe it was because I knew Vincent was watching.

Sounds stupid, I know.

Was he my lucky charm? Or did I just play my hardest because I wanted to impress him?

It was probably that.

But either way, I kicked ass.

Before the game, not wanting a ribbing from the entire team about my "new nerdy boyfriend," I'd put in my earpods and told them I needed to focus. And they'd pretty much left me alone. Thankfully, in the locker room after the game, it was a different mood.

Claps on the back, high fives, fist bumps, and cheers.

But then Peyton found me. He was wearing a shit-eating grin and he patted my cheek. "You trying to take my title?"

Peyton was the star quarterback, and he was by far the best player on the field. He was the king of Kings, but also a real nice guy so I knew there was no sting in his words.

"What title's that? Pretty boy? I don't think I qualify."

He laughed, totally at ease. "You've been on fire these last few weeks, man," he said. "I mean it. Whatever you're doing, you're doing it right."

The question was probably more whoever I'm doing . . .

"And keep doing it," he added. "I need to look good this year for the draft."

I snorted. He was going to be the number one pick. He knew it, we all knew it. Hell, everyone who followed college football on the western seaboard knew it. I gave him a bro handshake. "I got you."

I had every intention to keep *doing* my lucky charm for as long as I could. If Vincent was my lucky charm . . . Whatever he was, whatever we had going, I wanted more of it.

I really liked him. Maybe it was more than that. But it was complicated. He wasn't technically out of the closet. Except last night he'd said he didn't mind if people assumed he was gay, so . . .

Did that mean maybe an actual date could happen?

Sure, we'd hung out in public, but there was always a safe just-friends distance between us. It wasn't like we'd held hands or anything. Even though I'd wanted to.

God, how I'd wanted to.

And I wanted him to come to Shenanigans with me after the game. I wanted him to hang out with my friends so they could see how great and funny he was, but I knew he wouldn't be comfortable.

He wasn't ready for that.

So I spent a few hours at the bar missing him, wishing he was there. I was always down to celebrate a win and hang with the team and have a good time with friends. But there was an uneasy feeling tonight.

Like I had to split myself in two. One part of me for Vincent and one part for my friends.

I wanted them to join. I wanted to have both. I wanted to be able to celebrate a win and a fucking good game with the whole team and my boyfriend at the same time, dammit.

*Except he's not your boyfriend, idiot.*

A strong hand clapped me on the back. "You look like someone kicked your puppy."

It was Nate.

"I wish I could fucking drink," I said. "I'd be shitfaced right now."

He pointed his beer at me. "And that's why you can't drink." Then he gestured to the crowd, people dancing, music pumping. "You were the MVP today. Just don't tell Peyton I said that. You should be living it up, man."

I rolled my eyes and sighed. "You know, I think I'm just gonna go."

I went to sidestep him but he grabbed my arm. "Hey, wassup?"

"Nothing. Just shit I need to figure out."

His grip on my arm tightened and there was a seriousness to his gaze. "You do what you gotta do, but you can talk to me. Anytime, anywhere. Okay?"

I nodded.

"I mean it. Don't think for one second you're on your own. You've got a squad here eighty strong at your back, okay?"

I smiled at him. "Yeah, I know. Thanks. But this is on me. And it's nothing too heavy," I said, not wanting him to worry. I ran my hand through my hair. "It's just . . . complicated."

"Ah," he said with a knowing nod. "All that shit on social media, huh? I've seen it. Just ignore it, and they'll be posting shit about someone else in a day or two."

"It's not that. I mean, it kinda is."

*It's not really about the photos or whatever, it's about the person in the photos with me. And the fact that he's not here when I needed him.*

I didn't tell Nate that. It seemed I didn't have to.

He smirked and sipped his beer. "Then you should probably go see him."

I nodded quickly, trying not to smile. "Thanks, man."

I bailed, making my way to the bathrooms as a decoy, then slipping out the front doors when no one seemed to notice. Only a few people stopped me to say, "Great game," or "Hey, awesome play on the 20-yard line," or whatever.

I gave them my usual high five or fist bump but I didn't stop for conversation. There was somewhere else I'd rather be.

I didn't run back to the dorm, but one bonus of having a long stride was that I covered ground pretty quickly. I took the stairs to the second floor two at a time, trying not to be too desperate to see him.

It was so weird.

Once Nate told me to go see Vincent, there was nothing I wanted more. It was an excited urgency that pushed me down the corridor and fumbled my key in the lock. I swung the door open and burst into the room, dreading that he might not even be there . . .

But there he was, sitting on his bed, leaning against the head-board with his laptop on his thighs. He looked up at me and smiled.

So help me, I thought my heart might burst.

"Did you know that the first games of football were, for all intents and purposes, disorganized mobs of collegiates hellbent on violence and mayhem with a ball thrown in for good luck? And it wasn't until the 1880s that a semblance of law and order was introduced in the way of rules and things like line of scrimmage. And they changed the shape of the ball. It used to be round. Like a soccer ball."

I wasn't sure what he was saying but he sure looked cute saying it. "I didn't know that."

"And did you know that a middle linebacker, such as yourself, can burn up to three thousand calories on a training or game day. I'll never question how much you eat again. And I swiped these from the dining hall for you." He gestured to an apple, a bottle of juice, and some bread and jelly packets now sitting on my desk. "I wasn't sure if you'd have eaten enough after today's game—"

I laughed. "What are you doing?"

He looked at his laptop screen and shrugged. "I'm reading up on the game of gridiron football. I wanted to learn more about it, about what you do, more specifically . . ."

"You do?"

I couldn't explain how happy that made me.

I took off my jacket and tossed it onto my desk chair, then kneeled on his bed. I took his laptop and carefully set it aside, then grabbed his ankle like I did last time and pulled him down the mattress so I could lie on top of him.

He was laughing and I slid my arms underneath him and nuzzled my face into his neck, breathing him in.

Vincent wrapped his arms around me, widened his legs for me, and sighed. "What's this for?" he murmured.

"Just because."

He chuckled. "Okay."

"Because you went and looked up football stuff all on your own. You wanted to do that for me." I pulled one arm free so I could hold my head up. I wanted to look at his beautiful face. "That makes me happy. Thank you."

His eyes searched mine. "It's a fascinating game to watch. I can see why people enjoy it. The lady beside me in the audience—"

"Crowd."

"The lady next to me in the crowd screamed your name a lot. She'd jump and holler and then sit back down only to nudge me with her elbow and say things like, 'That Green 33 is really good,' and I'd just smile and nod, politely agree, but in my head I'm thinking, 'Girl, you've got no idea.'"

I laughed and traced my finger down the side of his face. "You didn't scream my name?"

Smiling, his eyes never left mine. "Not yet I haven't."

Jesus.

My dick twitched and I knew he felt it.

I ran my nose along the blush down his neck. I kissed his heated skin. "Hmm."

He was getting hard and ran his hand down over my ass and squeezed.

Holy shit.

"You played really well today," he breathed. "There's a

dichotomy of football-you and lover-you."

Lover.

I liked how that sounded. "Hm."

He craned his neck so I could kiss, lick, and suck. "Today I watched you smash men bigger than you. Football-you is fast and brutal." He groaned when I sucked his skin between my teeth. "But then lover-you, here with me right now, you're slow and gentle."

I slid my fingers under his shirt and ran my hand up along his ribs. His back arched, pushing against me, our erections pressed hard.

"Cobey," he breathed.

I sucked his earlobe into my mouth. "Yeah?"

"When will I be ready? I think I'm ready. I want . . ."

I pulled back and looked into his eyes, dark with lust. "You want what?"

His cheeks burst with color. "I want you to . . . I want to have sex. With you. I want you to be the one."

Oh god.

Every nerve ending in my body fizzed with heat and I crashed my mouth to his, kissing him deep. Our tongues met and he gripped my ass with both hands, grinding against me.

It almost did me in.

I wanted to be inside him. I wanted to bury myself in him, balls deep, and I wanted it so bad. It took every ounce of self-control I had not to agree and give him what he wanted.

But I had to put him first.

I ended the kiss by pulling his bottom lip between mine. I dropped my forehead to his, both of us breathing heavy. "I really want to do that. God, I want it so bad."

"But?" The look in his eyes almost made me give in . . .

"But . . . Uh, I have an above-average sized dick."

Vincent stared, then blinked, then stared again. And then he burst out laughing. "Uh, I would say that's an understatement. I haven't exactly seen any in real life, not including my own, but

I've watched my share of porn and I think if your football career doesn't work out, you can get a job in the adult entertainment industry."

That made me laugh, and I pecked his lips, happy that he wasn't offended or didn't feel rejected.

"I don't want to rush you," I whispered.

"You're not. You've been more than patient, but I'm ready." He nodded. "I think. You do have a really big dick."

I chuckled again. "Maybe we should work our way up to that," I suggested, kissing down his neck, nipping and biting. "Maybe we should see if you can come with my fingers in your ass."

His breathing hitched and his hips jerked involuntarily.

Oh yeah. He liked the sound of that.

I dragged myself down his body, lifting his shirt and biting at his nipple before I jumped off the bed. He laughed and rubbed at it, but as his eyes lowered to my crotch, his smile faded and he swallowed hard.

"Fuck," he whispered. "A hard-on in a suit."

Hmmm. I undid one button on my shirt, then another, and another, watching as his gaze followed my fingers, knowing he liked it. When my shirt was open, I popped the button on my suit pants, and Vincent slid his hand down to squeeze his dick.

I shucked out of my shirt and flipped the switch on my reading light, turned the overhead light off, and grabbed the bottle of lube from my bottom desk drawer. I tossed it onto the bed beside him.

"Stroke yourself," I urged. "I want to watch."

He was wearing his sweatpants so I pulled on the leg hem and helped him out of them. Then kneeling on the bed, I helped him out of his briefs as well. He held his cock, but even in the dimmed light, he was uncertain, clearly vulnerable.

I leaned over him, my nose almost touching his. "You are the sexiest thing I've ever seen." I widened his legs with my knees and he groaned. "I'm going to make this so good for you."

# NINE

## VINCENT

I'D WATCHED a lot of gay porn and I knew most of it was unrealistic and fake. I'd seen guys being fingered and I'd even experimented a little with my own ass so I knew it could feel good.

But the way Cobey did it?

The way he lay beside me, hooked my leg over his hip so he could finger me and kiss me at the same time. The way he'd watched my face, my eyes, looking for every cue I couldn't say. The way he'd watched as I'd stroked myself.

The way he'd made me come and how he'd watched as my orgasm raked through me.

How he'd come right after me and then held me.

How we'd fallen asleep in my bed wrapped around each other and woke up much the same way.

Was what Rafe had said true? Was Cobey in love with me? I wasn't sure. But was I in love with him?

I was certain I knew the answer to that.

And I'd never been in love before. Not really. I'd longed for and I'd admired from afar, but I'd never been in *love* love. It was tummy butterflies to the point of nausea, and heart palpitations and cold sweats.

It was soft kisses and belly laughs while we watched movies on his laptop. It was words of encouragement as I helped him with calculus. It was quick and dirty hand jobs before class.

It was him, a few days later, asking me to go to Shenanigans with him.

"To Shenanigans?" I'd tried to keep the horror from my voice, but from his smile, I think I failed.

He took the book out of my hand and set it aside, then laced our fingers. "I could tell you it was part of my socializing plan, but that would be a lie," he said. "I just wanna go out with you. I wanted you to come back to the bar after the game on Saturday but I knew there were too many people, and it can be pretty crazy after a win."

"You wanted me there?"

He nodded, and he honestly looked so vulnerable it did terrible things to my insides. "Yeah, I did. But I knew you wouldn't be comfortable with that crowd. But today's Wednesday, so it won't be that busy tonight. We can get dinner."

It sounded like a date.

"I did a hardcore weights session all afternoon and I'm starving," he added. "I'm paying because I'll be ordering the entire menu, so it's only fair."

His blue eyes met mine, and he let out a nervous breath. "It's okay, you don't—"

"I'd love to," I replied.

His whole face smiled. "Then hurry up and put your shoes on! I'm fading away here."

Two minutes later we were walking down to Shenanigans, and how happy it made him was so cute. If I'd known how much he'd wanted me to join him after the game and if I'd known he'd smile like that, I would have suffered the crowd and the stares.

"Their wings are so good, and the burgers are too. But they do a mean chicken steak." He talked of food the whole way there and I knew he was hungry. And excited. It was adorable.

"Okay, I'm trying to walk faster, but you've got longer legs than me."

He laughed and offered a fist bump and a first name greeting to the security guy at the door.

The waitress, who also knew Cobey by name, showed us to a booth. Cobey waited for me to slide in, like a freaking gentleman. I blushed, Gwen smiled, and Cobey grinned.

"Can I get you guys any drinks to start?" Gwen asked. Her short blonde hair was colored with chunks of teal and pink, her face kind and friendly.

*Maybe coming here isn't so bad.*

"Uh, Cobey's starving," I said. "So maybe we should let him order food right away. If that's okay?"

"Course it is," she replied with a dimpled smile. "Cobey, what'll it be tonight?"

As it turned out, he did order half the menu and I settled for chicken steak, salad, and fries. He ordered two sodas, and when Gwen left, Cobey was still smiling at me. It unleashed the butterflies in my belly, so I looked around the bar instead. It was decently busy. Most tables were full and I now realized that a few of them were watching us.

Oh boy.

"You okay?"

I looked right at him and smiled with courage I didn't feel. "Yep."

"First time in a bar?"

I nodded. "Yep. Clearly not yours. Does everyone everywhere know who you are?"

"Pretty much. I must have a memorable face or something."

"It has nothing to do with the fact that you're huge, incredibly good-looking, nice to absolutely everyone, and freakishly talented on the football field?"

He stared at me, eyebrow flicking slightly, a smirk on his lips. "You think I'm incredibly good-looking?"

I was glad for the neon lights and darkened room so he couldn't see me blush. "Yes."

"And freakishly talented on the football field?"

"Among other places."

His grin was smug. "Oh really?"

"Well, I've had very limited outside experience in that area, but I'm going to go with a yes. Very thorough, totally dedicated to the cause."

He laughed loud enough for people to turn and look, but thankfully Gwen arrived with our drinks and she blocked the view for most onlookers. "Your meals won't be long," she said, giving us both a cutesy smile before she went on her way.

Embarrassed, I sipped my drink. "People are watching us."

He turned to look, completely oblivious. He was always oblivious to how people looked at him. Then he looked at me and shrugged. "Don't worry about them." Then he stopped. "Oh, unless you want to get our meals to go . . ."

I shook my head. "No, no. It's fine. A month or two ago, I'd have probably said yes. But today it's okay."

"Ah, so you admit my tutorials have been working?"

"Well, the tutorials are more of a private matter, but you making me go out in public, like to the coffee shop or to the pier, that helps. And," I added with a shrug. "It helps that it's you. When I'm with you, I'm like a protected species. I'll admit, the scrutiny was hard at first, but either I'm getting used to it or people are now well aware that I'm a nobody and I'm no threat to them."

He cocked his head, his smile gone. "You're a what?"

"I'm a . . . I'm not on anyone's clique list, let's put it that way."

He frowned. "I don't know what a click list is."

"A clique, a tight-knit group of friends."

He chewed on the inside of his lip for a few seconds. "Please don't talk about my friend like that."

His friend . . . ?

"I wasn't talking about anyone else. I was talking about me."

"Yeah. My friend. Don't call him a nobody." He turned his soda around on the coaster a few turns, and I realized then that I'd honestly upset him. "If you called any of my other friends a nobody, I'd call you out, so why should I let you say it about you?"

"I, uh . . ." I felt well and truly rebuked, but in a warm and fuzzy kind of way. "I'm sorry. I won't do that again."

"Good. Because if you could see yourself." He sipped his drink. "Seems I still have more work to do."

I chuckled. "No, you don't. I said that out of habit. A mere reflex."

He looked right at me, into the very depths of me. "I know it was. That means I have more work to do. I wish there was the kind of technology where I could plug something into my brain and download it to you so you could see what I see."

Oh wow.

Okay, that one got me right in the heart.

"But there's not," he said, smiling now. "So we'll just have to do it the old-fashioned hard way."

"It probably doesn't help that you make that sound more fun."

He chuckled, and he leaned across the table, his eyes alight with mischief, and he was just about to say something when Gwen was back with a huge plate of buffalo wings and cheese sauce. There was no way to eat those with any kind of decorum.

"Uh, how are we supposed to eat these?"

"You've never had wings before?"

I shook my head. "Broke and on my own, remember?"

There was no shame or pity with Cobey. He simply put a plate in front of me. "Well, you're in for a treat. You just gotta dig in. It's messy, but that's kinda the point."

And he showed me how to tackle them. He must have eaten three or four to my one, but I didn't mind. "Are they good?" he asked, his hands and face a mess.

I laughed because I was sure I didn't look like that. And he didn't give a damn, not about what he looked like, not about what people might think. It was one of his best features. "Exceptional."

We'd barely gotten our faces and hands clean when our meals arrived and mine was massive. He'd be getting half of it, for sure. "I hope you're hungry."

He was already demolishing his Cajun chicken pasta, and he smiled as he chewed. "Pretty much all the time," he said with his mouth half-full, and I couldn't help it.

I laughed.

God, I was so in love with him.

Yep. There was no denying it. Head over heels.

It gave my heart flutters just to think that, to admit it to myself. It would probably end terribly, but for now, I was going to enjoy it. Well, I'd enjoy it for as long as he didn't know. That way there'd be only the endorphin and serotonin rush, not the awkwardness.

I could live with that.

I'd gotten through half my meal when he'd finished his pasta and I very gladly offered him my plate. "Had enough?" he asked. "It's probably more than I've ever seen you eat."

I leaned back to give my stomach some room. "More than enough. It was really good, but I'm done."

I watched as he had a few mouthfuls of salad. "You're playing away this weekend?" I asked.

He nodded and sipped his drink before he replied. "Yeah, UCLA Bruins on their home turf. It'll be a good game." Then he looked twice at me. "Did you wanna come? I can get you a ride."

"Oh no, thanks." I shook my head. "A trip up the freeway with strangers is how every horror movie starts."

He chuckled. "They wouldn't be strangers. My parents would take you."

I stared at him, trying to hide the real horror movie my face was probably making. "Oh, it's okay. Rafe's having another party on Saturday night and he asked me if I wanted to go. I'm thinking

I will actually go this time. You know, trying to be more sociable like my good tutor says."

He was clearly surprised. "You're gonna go?"

I shrugged. "Well, I thought I might. Just for a little while."

"Okay, that's cool." For the first time, his face was unreadable. "Yeah, you absolutely should go."

"I'd be home by ten, eleven tops," I said, for no apparent reason. His reaction made me nervous and I wasn't sure why. "I think our nerdy parties are significantly different from what you and your football friends probably call a party. Not that I'm truly certain because I've never been. To be honest, if I do show up, Rafe will probably require some form of cardiogenic shock therapy."

"What's that?"

I imitated holding two defibrillator paddles like they do on TV. "Clear."

He chuckled. "Right." Then he sighed, put down his knife and fork, and pushed the near-empty plate aside. "Vee, it's totally cool. You should go, spend some time with your friends. You might even have fun."

"Maybe. Not sure fun is the right word, but I'm trying . . . to, you know, put into action what you've been teaching me."

"Oh," he said. "Yeah, sure." He looked around, anywhere but at me. "I, um, I just have to go to the bathroom. Be right back."

Cobey was up and gone so fast, I wasn't sure what just happened. Was he mad at me? For what? Suggesting I do everything he's been trying to get me to do?

I was confused.

And I didn't really understand people at the best of times. I understood quantum physics better than I understood people.

And I thought I knew Cobey pretty well. And maybe I did. Maybe it was emotions clouding my perception . . .

Ugh. Why were emotions so persuasive?

I saw Cobey come out of the restrooms and he got halfway across the floor when a woman intercepted him. She wore a skirt and a short T-shirt. Clearly very drunk, she threw her arms around his neck, and he tried to peel her off him. "Whoa, Jayda, no thanks," Cobey said.

It made me feel . . . things.

Unease, mostly. Uncomfortable. Uncertain.

Why did she throw herself at him like that? Did this happen often? Not with her but with anyone? Had they hooked up before?

Oh god.

*What if they have?*

The unease in my belly turned sour.

Jayda then slid her arm around his waist, falling into him, all over him. I couldn't hear what she said exactly, but I heard Cobey just fine.

"I said no."

I might not have understood much when it came to the social rituals of people, but I understood that.

I was out of the booth before my brain could stop me, about to do what, exactly, I had no idea.

Cobey gave me an apologetic smile, but I was focused on Jayda. "Hi, Jayda, is it?"

She almost fell backward and Cobey had to catch her. Christ. "Hey, I know you," she slurred, looking at me.

What I was about to do, as it turned out, was lecture her on sexual coercion and not taking no for an answer, when I realized she was too intoxicated to reason with.

A guy came up to us. I remember him speaking to Cobey once, though I couldn't remember his name. All blond preppy guys tended to look the same. He was on the wrestling team. "Sorry, Green," the guy said. "I'll take her from here."

It wasn't his smarmy smile and it wasn't Cobey's lack of smile I noticed, it was how Jayda reacted. She clung to Cobey, trying to hide behind him almost, trying to make herself smaller.

I understood that too.

"No need," I said. "We'll make sure she gets home."

Mr. Smarmy Preppy Guy turned his attention to me. He clearly didn't like me, and it was mutual. Maybe I wouldn't have been so brave if I weren't with Cobey. But there was no way I was leaving her with him. He stared at me and I stared right back.

Before he could say anything, Cobey gave him a wide clap on the arm, making him look at Cobey instead of me. "It's all good, Gavin," Cobey said. "We already said we'd get her home. See you around, hey?"

Cobey put his arm around Jayda, more to hold her up than anything, and I didn't even mind. Now she looked a little wary and sad, so I took off my jacket and helped her into it while Cobey paid the tab. I didn't hear what he and Gwen talked about, even though they were just three feet away. It looked like she was saying thank you.

Jayda didn't say much on the way back to campus, except to say thanks and how Gavin was a slimeball and how sorry she was. It was only a short walk, but with her one step forward, three steps sideways, it took a lot longer than usual. She lived in the dorm next to ours and, thankfully, on the first floor. Her RA met us in the corridor.

Of course Cobey knew him too.

"Oh, thank god you're here," Cobey said. "I didn't want to dig through her pockets for keys."

"Oh dear," the RA said. "Someone's not going to be feeling too well tomorrow."

We got her safely into her room, Cobey gave the RA a brief rundown, and it wasn't until we were walking back to our dorm that I realized why I was cold. "Oh shoot. My jacket."

"Were your keys and phone in it?" Cobey asked.

I patted down my pockets. "No, I have those . . ."

"Here," he said, starting to take his zip hoodie off. "Are you cold?"

"No, I'm fine," I said, stopping him. "That's very sweet, but it's . . . it's just that's my only jacket, that's all."

Cobey frowned and slung his arm around me. "Come on, let's get you inside."

## COBEY

He had one jacket. Just one. It was a cool jacket; old denim, maybe it'd been black once, but it was gray now, worn-in and had an authentic vibe. The type you found at a really expensive store in LA. Or a lucky find in a thrift store. I didn't need to guess which one Vincent got it from.

His *only* jacket.

Man, I had a dozen hoodies, five different outer wear jackets, windbreakers, blazers and formal coats, and those were just the recent fashion kind. Hell, I even have a ski jacket from when I went skiing *once* a few years back. Probably cost two-hundred bucks and I wore it for one weekend.

Vincent was a constant privilege-check for me.

And to be honest, that was something most people I knew could use every once in a while.

Our dinner date had been going well. And yes, I thought of it as a date, even if it was unofficial. It hadn't ended exactly how I'd planned, but I was okay with that. I was just glad Jayda got home okay.

When she'd first come up to me, I thought it was weird. She was drunk and clingy, and then Vincent had come over to speak to her. He was different. Annoyed and defiant. Or something. It was weird enough, but then Gavin rocked up and said something smartass and Vincent stared him down like he was ten feet tall and bulletproof.

For a smaller, nerdy guy who hated crowds and being the center of attention, who was sweet and funny, Vincent sure had a feisty side.

Well, I didn't know if feisty was the right word. Like those cute little kittens that think they're as big and ferocious as lions? Kinda like that.

But still . . . I'd never seen Vincent angry.

He was quiet when we got back to our room. Just said he was tired, and when I pulled up my laptop on his bed to watch something like we usually did, all snuggled up together, it was only a few minutes in and he was asleep.

I stayed there for a bit longer, not wanting to wake him. I rubbed his back and kissed the top of his head, unable to shake the feeling that something had changed tonight.

And not in a good way.

Vincent and I needed to talk, that much was clear. We'd been fooling around for weeks, and where before it had felt as easy and natural as breathing, now it was . . . complicated.

Weeks of fun, good times, making out, and getting off but never talking about the important stuff.

Why did emotions have to mess things up?

The next morning, I was up before him. I wanted to get a decent run in before class to try and clear my head. I had a big game coming up at UCLA on the weekend and couldn't afford to fuck anything up.

I was going through my closet when Vincent woke up. He sat up and scrubbed a hand over his face. He took in my running gear, then reached for his phone. "What time is it?"

"Just after six."

He squinted. "What are you doing up?"

Couldn't sleep.

Worried sick.

Heartsore.

"I need to get a run in before practice today," I said, pulling out the hoodie I'd been looking for. I held it up for him to see. "This is the smallest one I've got. It's supposed to be cooler today, I think. Anyway, you can wear this until we get your jacket back. Or you can just have it forever. I don't wear it."

He squinted again and then put his glasses on. "Oh. Thank you."

I put it on the end of his bed. "I won't be at breakfast, sorry. Gotta run."

He frowned. "Okay."

I got to the door, feeling like shit, and stopped. "Hey, Vee?"

"Yeah?"

"Are we good?"

He squinted at me again, this time with his glasses on. Maybe I shouldn't have asked him that while he was still half-asleep. "Uh, yeah, of course," he said. "I'm good. Are you good?"

I nodded, even though I didn't feel good. "Yeah." I left him alone and hit the pavement running. And I ran and ran, keeping pace and measured breaths, running until my shirt was soaked through, my legs and lungs burned, and my mind was clear.

And I was doing so much better until I went back into our room, and on my desk was a croissant, an apple, and a juice box. Just sitting on the corner in a Vincent-worthy neat little pile.

Because he was worried I didn't eat enough, especially on training or game days.

I didn't know whether to laugh or cry.

I wanted to do both.

My heart squeezed, fluttered, and ached all at once. And my head was a jumbled mess all over again.

I showered real quick and sat through two classes that I didn't hear one word of. I was late to practice and I'd never been late. Ever. "Sorry, Coach," I said, running in.

But practice should have been good. The perfect stress reliever. I knew the motions, the plays. I knew the game. It was the only thing I *did* know.

And what did I do?

I missed tackles. I mistimed hits. I dropped the ball. Three times. Three fucking times. I got hit. I let my receiver get hit. I made the wrong call. I was out of breath and out of my goddamned mind.

My teammates had tapped my helmet the first few times I'd fucked up, but when I fumbled an easy ball, they were looking at me like I'd been possessed.

"Fuuuuuck!" I screamed, thumping the side of my own helmet.

"Dude, what the hell?" Jared cried.

"The fuck is up, Green?" Ricky asked. I was too pissed at myself to note the concern on his face.

"I don't fucking know!"

"Green!" Coach screamed across the field. "Sideline. Now."

I dropped my head with a sigh and tried to collect my temper. I jogged off the field, ignoring the eyes and the silence.

Fuck this.

I sat on the sideline, about six empty chairs between me and the nearest other guy. The coaching team gave me some space, peppered with concerned glances, and I knew I'd get an earful from Coach when this was over.

I'd be lucky to even start on Saturday's game.

Fucking hell.

After a long while, Coach did come over. He was a big guy, graying hair, sharp eyes. "Gonna take your helmet off?"

I shook my head. "Figure it might save my stupid fucking brain when I bang my head against a wall a hundred times."

He sighed. "So it's not your day, huh?"

I shook my head. "No."

"We all have shit days, son. All we can do is shake it off and get our heads right for the next one."

I nodded. "Okay."

He studied me for a bit and I kept my gaze firmly fixed on the field ahead. "Nate said you put in six miles before breakfast."

It was closer to eight, but whatever. "Yeah."

"You got something on your mind," he said. It wasn't a question. "You need to learn how to leave it at the gate. You've got the skills to make it, Green. And you know the scouts are watching you. It's a big game this weekend. UCLA on their home turf, and there will be eyes on you. Don't mess your stats up now."

I was still two years out from being drafted, but the NFL scouted talent and watched it grow until it was ripe for the picking. I knew how it worked. We all did.

I nodded.

"Don't fuck it up."

He was right. "Yes, sir."

He nodded toward the locker room. "Hit the showers. And I wanna see you before the game, you hear?"

I looked at him then. "Yes, sir."

I dragged my sorry ass to the showers and tried to scrub my bad mood away. Most of the guys came in and some clapped me on the back. Some said nothing. Some told me in no uncertain terms I needed to get my shit together for the sake of the entire defensive team.

They weren't wrong.

I grabbed my bag and wondered if a night of drinking would fix anything, knowing damn well it would not, when Nate found me. "Hey," he said gently. "Got a minute?"

I resisted sighing and followed him out. He walked for a bit, found a bench seat, and waited for me to join him. I sat down, dropping my bag between my feet. "I don't really wanna talk about it," I began.

"Fair enough," he said easily. "I've seen every game you've played for FU. Every training session, every weight session. You never complain, you never bitch and moan. When we're busted on the ground and Coach yells at us to get up one last time, you're the first one on your feet. And this year, you've been playing like the football gods blessed your ass. Every single game has been perfection. You've got some of the best defense game stats in the state, Cobey."

This wasn't the conversation I was expecting.

"But that?" he said, nodding back to the way we'd come.

"That was some of the worst shit I've seen since elementary school."

Aaaaand there it was.

I stared at him, and he laughed. "Fucking hell, Cobes. Did you wake up this morning and forget how to play?"

I couldn't help it, I chuckled. "Thought I'd try a new spray on my gloves. Teflon. You heard of it?"

He laughed. "That explains a lot."

My laughter became a sigh. "Fucking hell. What a disaster."

"Well, I'm glad you still have your sense of humor."

"Vincent's going to a party this weekend and I'm pretty sure he's gonna hook up with someone. I mean, that's the whole point of what we've been working through. Getting him some experience so he can do that . . . with someone else."

Nate blinked. "Okaaay. I thought you two were . . . official? You're pretty much inseparable. There're photos of you two together all over social media."

I groaned. "Don't remind me. And no, we're not official. Because I'm too gutless to ask, because what if he says no? And he should say no. He should be out there dating and hooking up. It's all new to him and he's a fucking catch. And he's not technically out yet. I mean, he is, kind of. Not really. And I don't want to put him in a position where he feels pressured because that shit is hard, man. And if he goes to this party, what if he does hook up with someone? I mean, what if he goes to bed with someone?" I pushed my hand against my stomach. "God, it makes me feel sick."

"You need to talk to him."

"I know. But I'm chicken shit. And I can't think of anything else. All day. Since last night. I barely slept. I was up early and I haven't been able to concentrate all day. Christ, is there such a thing as a prolonged aneurism or some shit?"

"There is a medical condition," he replied. "Causes confusion, inability to concentrate. Nausea, heart palpitations."

I nodded. "I have all of those. What is it? Is it bad?"

He laughed. "It's called being in love, Cobey."

I stared at him. "That's not funny."

"I'm being serious. You're so in love with him—"

I put my head in my hands. "I know I am! That's the fucking problem."

"You need to tell him."

"I can't. We're roommates. He's helping tutor me for calculus. If he rejects me, it'll make it too awkward and I'll be heartbroken, and imagine how useless I'll be on the field then! I'll fail calc and be off the team anyway, so I guess it won't matter."

"He won't reject you."

"You don't know that."

"True. I don't. There are no guarantees."

I stared at him. "That's not helping."

"I'm not going to lie to you, Cobey."

"So what am I supposed to do?"

"Start with something smaller."

"Smaller? What does that mean?"

"That before you announce your undying love for him and vision of wedding bells and a house in the hills, maybe you could try suggesting going steady."

"Going steady? What is this, the 1960s?"

"Boyfriends, Cobey. Ask him to be your boyfriend." He scowled at me. "Jesus."

"Shut up. I'm panicking."

He snorted out a laugh and dug his thumb and forefinger into his eyeballs. "Cobey, you know I consider you one of my closest friends, right? And you're awesome and I love you like a brother."

Oh god. Insult incoming in three . . . two . . .

"But if you don't sort this out with him before Saturday, you won't be playing. You won't be *able* to play. And Coach mighta been concerned about you today but I can tell ya, he'll be pissed at you on Saturday if you turn up like you did today."

"I know."

"You need to talk to Vincent. Today. Now, preferably." He checked his phone for the time. "Where would he be at ten past five on a Thursday?"

"Uh, library, I think? He's tutoring right now. Until five thirty."

Nate stood up. "Come on. Get your bag."

"Where are we going?"

He looked at me like I was crazy. Or stupid. "Dude, where do you think we're going? To talk to him."

"Now?"

"Yes, now." He picked my bag up and dumped it on my lap. "Get up."

He strode off in the direction of the library and I had to hurry to catch up. "This is a bad idea," I said. "What if it goes to shit?"

Nate stopped walking and met my gaze. "Then I will get you shitfaced tonight so you can wallow. Then you can move into the anger stage for the game, be full of rage to smash the entire UCLA team. If it goes well, which I'm pretty sure it will, then I'm assuming you and him will be having sex all night and you'll be all loved up. But either way, come game time, you'll be on fire."

He started walking again, and I had to hustle to keep up. "So this is all about the team and not about my own personal happiness?"

He considered this. "Yes. But your personal happiness is also intertwined with football. Something I hope Vincent understands."

"He does, yes. Well, I think he does. He admires the commitment it takes."

"Good."

"He'd never watched a game before, until he met me, I guess."

That earned me a side-eye. "Never?"

I shook my head. "Not interested. Until he watched us play. Then he studied the history and the diet requirements and certain stats on linebackers so he could understand what I do."

Another side-eye.

I shrugged. "He's a nerd. Loves data and numbers. I dunno. I just would've watched YouTube videos, but not him."

Shit. We were in the quad already. And then we were at the door . . .

"Stop, Nate." I stopped walking, my heart in my throat. "What if he says no?"

"He watched you play one game and wanted to understand the science behind the sport so he could understand you. He did that *for you*. He's not going to say no."

"It was two games. The first game he just watched for the tight pants."

Nate tried not to smile as he pushed the door and waited for me to go first.

Goddammit.

There were people at tables, all being studiously quiet, with their noses in books. It's what I should be doing, given I had exams coming up and . . .

There he was.

Sitting with a girl, pointing to something on her iPad and nodding. His hair looked like he'd run his hand through it a hundred times, kinda flopping down onto his forehead. He wore his glasses, which made him ten times hotter. His black jeans and high-top Converse were his standard attire, but heaven help me . . . he was wearing my hoodie.

Seeing him in my clothes just did something to me.

It was the one I'd given him this morning, my faded purple Franklin U hoodie from last year. I didn't wear it because it was a bit small for me but still too big on him, and he had the sleeve cuffs rolled once. He looked so comfortable and warm, and I wanted to lay on his bed with my head on his chest and close my eyes—

"You okay?" Nate said beside me. He followed my line of sight. "Christ, you've got it bad."

My nerves exploded in my belly. "Uh, he's busy. I don't want to interrupt him while he's working."

Then Rafe appeared, carrying an archive box. "Oh hey, Cobey," he said, loud enough that Vincent turned to look.

Fuck.

"I'm glad you're here," Rafe said, motioning us to walk to his desk. He put the box down and opened up a planner. "A tutoring appointment freed up. If you want it, it's yours."

Oh.

"Oh."

"He won't need it," Vincent said, suddenly standing there. "Sorry, Rafe. I meant to tell you to take his name off the waitlist." But then he shot me a look and frowned. "Unless he wants to take it?"

"No!" I answered quickly. "No, no. It's fine." Shit. I didn't want Vincent to get into trouble. "Yeah, I, uh. I've been doing this thing? It's, um . . ."

"He hired a private tutor," Vincent said, as easy as pie.

Rafe looked between us. "Hm. Private, huh?" He took the magazines out of the archive box and gave Vincent a curious smile. "I'll just go file these."

We watched him leave, then Vincent turned to me. "You're a terrible liar."

"I know. So bad."

Nate laughed. "I've never seen you struggle like you have today."

"Gee, thanks," I said. Then, because Vincent and Nate were just left staring at each other, I thought it best to introduce them. "Vincent, this is Nate. Nate, Vincent . . . obviously."

They shook hands. "It's nice to finally meet you," Nate said.

"Likewise." Then Vincent cast his eyes on me. "What are you doing here? Is everything okay? What were you struggling with today? Are you okay?"

Then he noticed my forearm, or more importantly the red welt on it.

"Holy shit," he hissed, gently taking my arm for a closer look. "What happened?"

"I got tackled."

"He got annihilated," Nate added. "Smashed, many times. Worst training session he's ever had. Which is why we're here."

Vincent frowned. "Why? You went for a run this morning and then practice. Did you eat enough? Because your kilojoule expenditure—"

"Yeah, I'm fine. It's not that," I said. "I just . . . Christ." I turned to Nate. "This was a terrible idea." Then back to Vincent because I was entering panic mode. "I'm sorry. You're working."

"No he's not," Nate said.

We all turned back to the table he'd been sitting at to find the girl, a pretty blond freshman, getting up from the table. She'd packed up her stuff, had her phone to her ear, a bright smile, and she waved to Vincent and mouthed "thank you" before she hurried out the door.

I turned back to Vincent, about to apologize again, but he was already looking at me. "Cobey, what's wrong? You're starting to freak me out. Is everything okay?"

Oh god.

Here goes nothing.

"Not really. I've been going crazy all day. Well, actually, since last night. When you said you wanted to go to that party this weekend. Which is fine. I have no problem with that. I just don't want you to hook up with anyone else. The thought of that makes me want to punch something or vomit. Probably both. And I know—"

"I'm sorry, what?" Vincent's eyes were wide. He glanced around as if someone could hear. "You don't want me to *what*?"

"To hook up with someone," I mumbled. "Or go home with them. Oh god." I had to push my hand against my stomach.

Vincent blinked a few times. "Wh-why would you think I would do that?"

"Because you said you wanted to practice what I've been teaching you."

"Yeah. How to be a normal human being and talk to people."

Pretty sure Vincent was now mad. "And considering this conversation, I'm beginning to wonder which of us is the student."

Nate snorted.

Hold up. "You don't want to kiss other people?"

"Absolutely not."

I almost sagged with relief. "Oh, thank god."

"Wait. Do you?"

"No! Hell no. Just you. No one else."

"Good."

"Good."

"Good," Nate added. When we both looked at him, he sighed. "Look, guys. This has been real cute and somewhat painful to witness, so I'm just going to help you along here. Remember back in middle school when your friend would go up to the person you liked and asked them out for you?"

I wanted to die.

Vincent shook his head. "Not really."

Nate wasn't swayed. "Vincent, what Cobey really wants to know is if you'd be comfortable being exclusive with him, which may or may not include the word boyfriend. However labels are something you can discuss later, but right now he needs to know if you're amenable to dating, being serious, exclusive, going steady."

I stared at Nate, horrified. But also, "Dude, it's not the 1960s. I don't think people 'go steady' anymore. That's something my grandparents would say."

I could feel Vincent's gaze on me. "Cobey?"

I spun to face him. Trying not to panic. Trying really hard not to panic. "Um. Well, that was more words than I would've used but, uh, yes? What he said. I think?"

He pressed his lips together but a smile won out. A deep blush colored his cheeks. "Cobey, I . . ."

"If you don't want to, that's fine," I said.

It was not fine.

It was anything but fine.

I would probably crawl into a hole and become a hermit for the rest of my days.

"I mean, it would suck but I'd respect your decision. From my hermit cave."

Vincent chuckled and took my hand. "I'm assuming the exclusivity clause applies to you too," he said, still smiling.

"Yes, of course! God, yes. Only you. Since the day we met, it's only been you."

His eyes met mine, dark, intense, happy. "Then yes, Cobey. Dating, being serious, exclusive, whatever you want to call it. Going steady." He gave Nate a shrug. "I can respect that term."

Nate slapped me on the back. "You're welcome."

I laughed, relieved and so freaking happy. "You mean it?"

He nodded, laughing, so I threw my arms around him and hugged him, almost lifting his feet off the ground and probably holding him a bit too tight because he squeaked.

I set him back down, and fuck, I wanted to kiss him so bad but had to stop myself. That was a huge public step for someone who wasn't publicly out, and I had to remind myself that he wasn't ready for that. And that was perfectly okay. I mean, we'd just hugged, but people can hug without it having to mean anything—

But Vincent slid his hand around my neck and, leaning up on his toes, pulled me down for a kiss. Kinda sweet, kinda filthy, all kinds of hot.

Until someone squealed and several people clapped and whistled.

We broke apart, Vincent's cheeks were flushed red, and we turned to find everyone in the tutoring center watching us. Some tables were empty, but most weren't. Rafe was holding a pile of magazines, a stunned smile on his face. Nate laughed, picked his bag up, and walked toward the door.

"See ya tomorrow at practice, Cobes," he said without turning around. He pushed the door open and called out, "You're welcome, everyone."

I couldn't help but laugh, and Vincent ducked his head. He hated being the center of attention, and this was a whole lot of that. "Wanna get out of here?" I asked quietly.

He nodded, so I led the way and didn't stop until we were almost at our dorm. Then, like he couldn't wait, he was pulling me up the stairs and into our room.

With the door closed and the outside world a million miles away, I knew we should talk. We both had things to say, questions to ask, and feelings to talk about. Well, I certainly had things I needed to talk about now that I wasn't such a hopeless mess.

But Vincent closed the distance between us with fire and determination in his eyes. He cupped my face and pulled me in for another kiss, confident, desperate, his tongue in my mouth until I groaned.

"I want you," he murmured against my lips. "I want you inside me."

# TEN

## VINCENT

COBEY CUPPED MY FACE, his eyes searching mine. "Are you sure?"

"I've never been surer. About anything." I pulled his shirt over his head. His huge chest, muscular and broad . . . had more red marks. I skimmed my hand over them. "Cobey."

"I got smashed at practice," he said. "All I could think about was you maybe hooking up with some other guy and, honestly, it wrecked me."

I slid my hand along his jaw and leaned up to kiss him. "I would never. Only you."

His grin was magnificent. "Only you too, Vee. I just wish I'd had the guts to talk to you before I got my shit clapped at practice."

I bit my bottom lip to stop from smiling too hard. "I'm sorry you had a shitty day."

With his hands on my neck, he kissed me. Slower this time, slower, but so much hotter. He began to lift the hem of my hoodie. "Ugh," he said, breathless. "Seeing you wear my clothes does something to me. I want you naked, but damned if I want to take this off you."

I laughed and pulled it over my head. "Naked, please."

He skimmed his hands over my chest, over my collarbone, up the back of my head into my hair, gently tugging my head back so he could kiss my throat. "You're so fucking hot," he murmured.

Then he raked his blunt fingers down my back to my waist and my ass. He pulled my hips to his, cupped my ass and squeezed, sending jolts of electricity through me.

I hitched one leg up and he held the back of my thigh, hoisting me up. I wrapped my legs around him, feeling the rigid length of his cock.

Wanting it.

Needing it.

Knowing I was going to get it.

*God, Vincent. You're going to get it. He's gonna bury that huge cock in your ass tonight. You're going to lose your virginity.*

He lowered me onto my bed, and pressing his full weight on me, he kept kissing me, rocking us, rubbing us.

It was glorious.

It felt so fucking good.

But I was still far too dressed. While my feet were in the air and I could reach them, I tried to pull my shoe off. "Not naked," I said with a grunt when my Converse wouldn't come off.

Damn the laces.

Cobey chuckled and leaned back, sitting on his haunches. He held my foot. "Impatient?"

"Yes." When I realized he wasn't undoing the stupid laces, I tried to pull at them.

He just laughed, but thankfully took the hint.

Socks and shoes finally gone, he skimmed his hands up my thighs, palming my erection but going for the button and fly. He undid them and began to pull them down, but stopped.

"Are you sure?" he asked. Then he leaned over me, his face a few inches from mine. "Do you want this?"

"Yes."

He kissed me soft and sweet. "I'm going to take my time to get you ready, so you gotta be patient, okay?"

I nodded.

With that, he pulled my jeans off. "Get into bed," he whispered. He jumped off and switched on his reading light before he made sure the door was locked and turned off the overhead lights. He took the lube and foil packet from his desk and threw them next to me on the bed before he proceeded to fully strip.

The condom made it so real. This was really happening . . .

And sweet mercy, his erection was so impressive.

*Holy shit, he's gonna fuck me with it, bury the whole thing inside me until I split open . . .*

*He won't hurt me. This is Cobey. Relax. Take a breath.*

"Are you okay?" he asked. He looked down at his cock; I must have been staring. "You look worried."

Uh, great.

"Just trying to remind myself to breathe."

Cobey's face softened and he climbed into bed with me and pulled up the covers. He leaned up on his elbow and studied my eyes. "If you want to stop at any time, you say stop, and I'll stop. If it's too much, we stop. We can practice more and try again another time."

"Okay."

He leaned down and kissed me. "And I'll remind you to breathe," he whispered with a smile.

He kissed me again, his hand wandering down my side to my hip, to my dick. He gave me a few long strokes while his tongue teased mine, and I was soon lost to how good it felt.

Even when he was lubing me up and stretching me, sliding his fingers in and out, first one, then two, I was imagining it was his cock.

I wanted it so bad. I was desperate to have him. Even though he'd told me to be patient, and I did trust him, but . . .

"Cobey, please." I pulled at my hair, writhing at his touch, trying to push down on his fingers. "Need you now."

He grunted and pulled his fingers out, kneeling in between my thighs. I undid the condom for him and he rolled it down his length. He applied more lube and hissed as he rubbed it all over his cock. "Fuck," he murmured. Then he leaned over me and kissed me. "You probably have some vision of me being perfect at this and making this amazing for you," he said. "But Vincent, baby. I'm so turned on right now this is likely to be over pretty quick. Just so you know."

I couldn't help but chuckle. I put my hand to his cheek. "I'll take whatever you can give me."

He crushed his mouth to mine, delving his tongue in deep as he hooked one of my knees up toward his chest. He broke the kiss to bring up my other knee and he held me like that, his cock pressing against my hole.

And he kept his eyes glued to mine as he pressed into me. Slow and breaching, stretching and burning, and I sucked back a breath, gasping as he tried to push in.

I wasn't sure I could take him. Not even a little bit. Not at all.

But then he made a pained sound, a soft whine, and his eyes were full of fear and wonder. And I was so captured by him, by the sounds he made, the way he looked at me, everything else seemed to fall away. Until there was a push as his cockhead slipped in, and then a slower glide as his cock entered me.

"Oh my god, Vincent," he breathed. He kissed me, tongue, lips, and ragged breaths. He pulled out a little only to push back in, deeper this time. Then he did it again, and again. Slow and gentle, he was so far inside me.

I was so full of him. I felt like I might split apart, and it was a strange intrusion at first. But it also felt good, in an odd way. And the more he moved, the better it felt.

I scraped my nails down his back and he arched and let out another pained cry. "Fuck, Vincent. I'm trying not to come and you do that to me."

I took his face in my hands, making him look at me. "Come. I want to feel it."

He smashed his mouth to mine in a bruising kiss, rough and deep. He filled me at both ends, so completely. He wrapped his arms underneath me, held me tight, and thrust into me, hard enough that I gasped into his mouth.

And he cried out, his cock swelling harder, buried to the hilt, and I felt him come.

He thrust hard and flexed, his whole body tight, his face filled with ecstasy as his orgasm rocketed through him. The sounds he made . . . my god, such beautiful sounds.

All I could do was hold on and bring him in for another kiss as his body twitched, until he collapsed on top of me, completely spent. Still inside me, I never wanted him to leave.

I rubbed circles on his back and kissed the side of his head.

"Holy fuck, Vee," he whispered. He pulled out of me slowly, rid himself of the condom into the trash, then scooped me up into the biggest, tightest hug. "You okay?"

My legs felt a bit weird from being up near my head, I assumed, and my ass felt stretched and empty. I nodded into his neck but he clearly wasn't convinced. He pulled back, cupping my face. "Are you okay, Vincent? Christ, did I hurt you? I'm sorry I never made you come—"

I chuckled and silenced him with a kiss. "I never expected to," I said. "It was my first time. I was expecting pain, to be honest."

He frowned. "There should never be pain."

"There wasn't. It didn't hurt. Despite the size of your dick. You took very good care of me."

He almost smiled. "I'm sorry. Are you sad? Or mad at me?"

"What? Why would I be?"

"I just wanted it to be . . . good. I dunno. Special."

"It was," I whispered, raking my hand through the hair at his temple. "It was more than just sex for me, Cobey. It was with you, for a start. But it was intimate and sweet, and it means a lot to me." I kissed him. "And I'm no longer a virgin, so there's that."

That made him smile.

The truth was, for me at least, there'd been an exchange of

something special. I gave him my body, my first time, and all my trust. And he took it like the gift it was.

He already had my heart, so . . .

"So are we doing the exclusive thing for real?" he asked. His eyes searched mine, and while there was vulnerability in his, I hoped he saw only surety in mine.

"For real."

He grinned, kissing me again. "I really like you, Vee."

God, my heart was thumping. "I really like you too. And I'm sorry you thought I was going to hook up with someone new at the party. I just meant I was going to try to talk to people, that's all. My god, I couldn't imagine doing what we just did with some random stranger."

He tightened his hold on me. "Me either. I kinda freaked out. I didn't know what we were. We've been doing all this stuff and never talked about what any of it meant."

With my hand on his cheek, I kissed him again. "It's meant the world to me," I whispered. "Everything you've shown me. Every touch, every kindness. I've never known physical intimacy before. Not even a hug, really. I never realized how amazing it could be. You showed me that."

His eyes swam. "Oh, Vee. I want to show you everything." He pressed his lips to mine, fierce and full of emotion, and then he pulled me into the crook of his neck. His whole body enveloped me. Muscular, masculine. Strength, warmth, comfort.

He was one hundred percent sex.

"Hmm." Running his hands down my body, he slipped his hand between us and wrapped his hand around my dick. "You're hard. Seems I have more to show you tonight."

I laughed out a groan as he stroked me. "Everything about you turns me on. Being naked with you, having you inside me. I may not have come then, but thinking about it now . . ."

Cobey groaned. "Jesus, Vee. You'll make me want to go again." He rolled me onto my back, spread my legs with his knees, and kissed me with smiling lips. "How about I just make you come instead?"

"I was quite content to just lie here with you," I said, but then he sucked my cock into his mouth, pressing a finger into my still-lubed ass. It was sensory overload in the best of ways. "Oh god, yes." He curled his finger and struck a live wire inside me, again and again, igniting sparks on every nerve ending as he took me into his throat.

I came so hard.

So fucking hard.

The room was still spinning and I hadn't yet come back into my body when Cobey lay down on me and wrapped me up in his arms. We pulled the blankets up, snuggled down, and fell asleep.

## COBEY

I woke up hungry, hot, and horny.

That in itself was no great surprise. It was how I woke up most days. But I'd slept in Vincent's bed again and woke up with his ass pressed against my morning wood. It was also hella hot with his body heat, and I was starving.

I reached over him and grabbed my phone. It was 6:00 a.m. and it was game day. Unless eating ass and sucking cock counted as a meal, which I was highly doubtful it did.

"Hey, Vee?" I said, tapping his hip.

Nothing.

So I grabbed his hip and rubbed my dick against his ass crack.

"Hmm," he groaned sleepily.

Now he was awake.

"I need food."

He froze, and he was quiet for a second. "What?"

I snorted. Sleepy Vee was so cute. "Food. I'm starving."

He groaned for real this time, burying his face into the pillow. "Thought I was about to get fed. Was having the best dream."

I burst out laughing. "Maybe later. It's game day. And I'm starving. My stomach thinks my throat's been cut and is sending emergency beacons to my brain."

Vincent chuckled into the pillow. "Then go eat."

"You have to come with me." I climbed up and over him, jumping off the bed. I took most of the blanket with me, leaving a very naked Vincent lying very naked and gorgeous.

And did I mention naked?

He was face down, his slim and pale body, the outline of ribs, his trim waist, and the swell of his ass.

"Jesus, you are a fucking snack," I said, kneeling back on the bed and kissing up his spine. "I could just eat you."

He laughed and tried to roll over, which was a bit hard with me all over him. "Help me up," he said. "We need to feed you. I'm not having Nate track me down again because you're not playing well."

Grinning, I helped him to his feet and I didn't miss the way he winced. Oh shit. "Are you sore?"

He wiggled his ass. "Not really. Just . . . I can feel where you've been." He shrugged. "I kinda like it."

I laughed and had to give my dick a squeeze. I was fully naked and he watched me do it.

"Christ, Cobey," he breathed. His eyes met mine, pupils blown, his lips parted, his tongue right there . . .

I shook my head out of the Vincent-haze and put my finger up. "Nope, Mr. Sexy As Fuck, don't look at me like that. I need a piss, food, shower, in that order, then maybe a pre-game orgasm. Then maybe some more food."

He laughed. "Charming."

But thankfully he didn't argue. We threw on some clothes, me just any old thing, I did not care. Vincent wore my old FU hoodie that he wore the day before. And after a quick bathroom stop, we headed to the dining hall.

It was early, and there were only a few others at far tables. I piled my plate high and Vincent grabbed some toast and fruit with his coffee. He even ate some of it before he pushed it toward me.

"You don't eat enough," I said.

"I never have," he replied, sipping his coffee. "But I also don't expend anywhere near as much energy as you."

I grinned at him. "We can work on that."

He blushed behind his coffee cup. "I hope so."

Damn.

How the hell was that so hot?

How the hell was *he* so hot? With his floppy dark hair, heated blush on his pale skin, glasses. All I could think about was last night. What he looked like, the way he looked at me when I entered him.

What he felt like.

And now that I'd been inside him once, I wanted to do nothing else.

"Goddammit," I mumbled. "Maybe I should have had breakfast on my own. Every time I look at you, I picture last night and how good it was, and I want to bend you over this table."

He stared at me, his coffee cup stopped almost at his lips. "Fuck, Cobey."

"Sorry, I—"

His gaze fixed on mine, heated, turned on. "What time do you need to leave for the game?"

"Oh hey, Cobey," someone said, startling me as they came up behind me. It was Alex from the swim team. I'd noticed him and his teammates around campus and at Shenanigans too. Because let's be real, a swimmer's physique wasn't exactly a chore to look at.

"I would not recommend the eggs today. Too rubbery." Those guys packed away the food like we did.

"Noted!" I replied, giving him a fist bump.

"Good luck today!"

"Thanks, man."

He walked off and someone else yelled out. "Kick some UCLA ass, Green." I turned to see Grimes from the lacrosse team give me a nod.

Christ.

I turned back to Vincent. "Maybe we should go."

He just laughed. "I'll just grab something to take with us."

"You should have eaten more."

"It's not for me. It's so you don't need to come back down to get more food. That way you can spend more time doing me."

I grinned at him. "So it is for you."

"By proxy."

I stood up and took my tray. "I don't know what that means but I'm just gonna agree."

Vincent grabbed some fruit, a water, and some baked pastry thing, and he was all smiles as we walked out. And man, I couldn't wait to get him back to our room.

Well, until we were halfway back and my phone rang. It was Nate.

"Hey," he said when I answered.

"Hey, man."

"I was just calling to see how things went with Vincent. And if we have our linebacker today."

I snorted. "You will certainly have your linebacker on his game today."

"So things went well . . ."

"Things went very well." Vincent was looking at me funny so I shrugged and told him, "It's just Nate. He wanted to see how we ended up."

He made an embarrassed smiley face and his cheeks went red. It made me laugh.

"Oh, if you're with him now," Nate said, "tell him to ignore all the shit online. They're just jealous. Cobey, my guy, I will see you at eight thirty at the bus."

I stopped walking. "What shit online?"

Nate was quiet. "You haven't seen it? Look, man, it's just the usual, more of the same shit they've been posting for weeks. Ignore it, Cobes. What does Coach say about that online shit?"

"That it ain't real. That it's just people saying shit they don't have the balls to say to your face."

"Exactly."

Vincent was standing in front of me, looking up at me. "You okay?"

I gave him a nod. "Yeah, okay, Nate. See ya at the bus."

I disconnected the call and went straight to my socials.

"What is it?" Vincent asked.

"Ugh. Nate said to ignore the shit online. For you to ignore it, he said. Which makes me think it's about you. Not me."

I scrolled, and sure enough, there were photos . . . "Us, in the tutoring center," I said. I turned my phone around to show him the photo of us talking, faces close, smiling, hugging.

Kissing.

Fucking hell.

Then I read the comments. "Cobey Green is officially off the market . . . Half of Franklin U weeps . . . Who the FU is that Vincent guy . . . Vincent who? I give it a week . . ." I looked up at him. "I'm so sorry. Why would they be hating on you? Can't they be happy for us? God, it's not right. I don't care what they say about me. But not you. They can't say shit about you."

"Hey," he said quietly, smiling up at me. "I don't care about any of that. And you shouldn't either."

"How can you not?"

"What happens on social media doesn't concern me. Unless it's libelous, I couldn't care less, and to be honest, I'd rather not know. Except that photo was cute. Could you send it to me?"

I rolled my eyes but couldn't help but smile. Most people would be freaking out right now—and I'd learned long ago to let the negative comments go—but there was Vincent, not giving one single fuck.

Then he whispered, "I think we should shower first. But you

gotta make it quick. We have other important matters to tend to before you need to leave."

So I showered, trying not to think about whatever it was Vincent had in mind for me. And also trying not to think about those stupid online comments. It really pissed me off, and it wasn't a good mindset to be playing football.

I threw my toiletry kit onto my desk and threw my towel at the hook. Vincent was sitting on his bed, dressed in sweatpants and a T-shirt, towel-drying his hair.

"What's wrong?" he asked, clearly picking up on my mood.

"Nothing, sorry. I just . . . those comments piss me off."

He stood up and gently hung his towel and leaned up to kiss me. He was all toothpaste and shower clean and warm. I deepened the kiss with a groan, holding his jaw and pulling his hips to mine.

I could have kissed him like that all damn day, but he pulled away. He took my hand and walked backward until he was sitting on the edge of his bed again. I wanted to follow him onto the mattress, settle myself between his legs, and . . .

"You need to focus," he said, looking up at me.

Uh, what? "What?"

"It's game day." He eyed my crotch. It was right at his eye level. He pulled at the drawstring on my shorts.

Oh, I liked where this was going.

"Yes, it is."

He pulled the waistband down. "Ignore all the social media shit. They don't matter today."

I shook my head. "They don't matter."

He slid my cock out of my boxer briefs. "You need to focus on your game play and strategies."

"Fuck yes, I do."

He fisted the base and gave me a slow stroke. "You have a job to do."

I could barely nod, let alone speak.

Then he licked the underside, tonguing the frenulum. "You're going to be the best linebacker on the field."

I nodded again.

He tapped the head of my cock on his bottom lip. "Say it."

"I'm gonna be the best linebacker. Jesus, Vincent, please."

He looked up at me as he opened wide and took me in. His warm, wet mouth, his cruel tongue, torturing me. He jerked me off as he sucked me, so good, for the longest time before he slipped his other hand in to cradle my balls.

I grabbed his head, fisting his hair. I wanted to fuck his face, deep as I could. I wanted to get lost forever. I wanted to . . .

"Fuck, Vee. Gonna come."

So he sucked harder and fingered my balls. I don't know if he did that accidentally or not, but it sent me.

It sent me to fucking heaven.

I came, shooting hard, and he took it. He drank it all. We'd given each other head a few times, but this was the first time he'd swallowed . . .

Holy fuck.

The room spun, dark and dizzy. The only thing I could hear was my blood pounding in my ears. I think I swayed.

Vincent chuckled, holding onto me. "You okay?"

It took a second, but I finally found my voice. "I feel invincible."

He laughed again, clearly proud of himself. "I must've had a good tutor."

I held his face and kissed him, going to my knees between his legs. I pushed him back so he was lying down, then pulled his legs so his ass was just off the edge of the mattress, and his dick was right in front of my face.

I pulled him free and took him straight into my mouth. No teasing, no licking, no warning.

His back arched and I held his hips as I took him into my throat. He cried out, lifting one leg up onto my shoulder, and I took him in to the hilt, my nose nestled in his pubes.

He let out a rasping whine as he came, his whole body contorting while I held his hips and swallowed around his pulsing dick.

I left him slumped on his bed, curled into a smiling, sated ball. I kissed the side of his head, took my gym bag—and the snacks he'd taken from the dining hall—and went to meet the team.

When Coach saw me, he studied me as I bit into the apple. "You good today, Green?"

I grinned at him as I chewed. "Never better."

Nate laughed beside me and Peyton clapped me on the back.

"Let's go, Kings!" someone called out as we boarded the bus.

I was pumped, itching to get on the field.

*Let's fucking go.*

# ELEVEN

## VINCENT

I LAY there for a time wondering if it was possible for sex to wipe your brain.

I was beginning to think it might be.

I must have dozed off because my phone buzzed with a message and it woke me up. I didn't get messages too often, so I snatched up my phone to see who it was.

I smiled when I saw Cobey's name.

*Hey. You okay? You weren't too good when I left.*

I snorted and typed out a reply. *I'm very okay, thanks to you.*

He replied with an angel emoticon.

*I'm on the bus headed to UCLA. The guys are giving me shit. Apparently I'm too happy.*

I wanted to hug my phone. *Should I be sorry?*

*LOL no.*

I sighed happily. *You're going to kick ass today.*

*Bringing home the W for sure.*

The W? I tried to think of what that could mean.

*It means the win, in case you didn't know.*

I snorted. *Thanks. Guess I'll need to learn football-speak. Or sport-speak in general.*

*I'll add it to my list of things to teach you.*

*Mmm. I'll look forward to that.*

God, was this text-flirting? Were we flirting? Was this sexting? It made me all giddy and stupidly excited.

The text bubble appeared and disappeared again, and I waited for his reply.

*I'm trying not to think about what you mean.*

*Sorry.* Because that was a blatant lie—I was not sorry at all—I was considering adding a wink or a devil emoji when his next text came through.

*What are you doing right now?*

*Still in bed.*

*Fuck. Vincent. Not helping.*

I sent him back the angel emoji, then I added *I fell asleep because someone wiped me out.*

*LOL you're welcome.*

Not sure what else to add, I typed out *Kick ass today, and have fun. See you tonight.*

His reply took a few minutes. The text bubble appeared and disappeared a few times.

*Go to the party tonight. Have lots of fun. And if some really hot guy hits on you, what will you tell him?*

*The odds of that happening are minuscule.*

*Vincent.*

*To be honest, I wouldn't even be aware he was hitting on me.*

Because that was the god honest truth.

My phone rang in my hand, startling me. Of course it was Cobey. I answered with a laugh. "I wouldn't know what to say because I wouldn't even be aware he was interested. You know I have no clue about these things."

He sighed. "Oh, Vincent."

The way he said my name, all gruff and breathy, it settled

something warm in my belly. It made me all fuzzy and strangely nervous.

"The odds of me even speaking to anyone other than Rafe are also slim to none. I'm more of a keep my head down and don't speak to anyone kind of guy. As you know. So no, I don't know what I'd say if some guy tried to hit on me." I grimaced and covered my eyes with my free hand. "Shit, Cobey. What do I do? Maybe I shouldn't go."

"Yes, you should totally go. Spend some time with your friends. And," he said, "if someone tries to hit on you, you look them right in the eye and say, 'Sorry, I already have a boyfriend.'"

There was muffled cheering from Cobey's end, and I could picture his entire team heckling him.

Boyfriend.

He said boyfriend.

I was grinning at the ceiling, at the ridiculous Mary-Jesus-Adam-Driver poster, trying to hold the side of my face so my enormous smile didn't break my face.

"Okay," I whispered with a laugh. "Boyfriend."

I TOOK MY BOOKS DOWNSTAIRS, and in trying to be more social, I decided to sit out in a shady spot in the quad instead of hiding in the library. The sun was shining, the sky a pretty blue overhead, and there was even a gentle breeze. Birds chirped and people talked and laughed.

Did it always look so nice out?

Or was it just because I was in such a good mood? It absolutely was and I knew it, and even though I knew better than to hinge my own happiness on someone else, I let myself revel in it.

To be absolutely head over heels for someone and have them feel the same way? To be appreciated and wanted? That shit felt good.

I knew myself, and I didn't need Cobey's affection to validate my worth.

But man, hearing him call me his boyfriend set my heart on high.

He made me really happy.

Love was a crazy drug. Like taking serotonin, oxytocin, endorphins, and dopamine and giving them an electrical charge of 240 volts.

Just crazy.

"Oh, Vincent? Is that your name?"

I looked up to find a woman in front of me and it took me a second to remember where I'd seen her. She looked vastly different now, wearing jeans and a sweater, and very sober. "Oh, Jayda," I said. "Yes, I'm Vincent."

"I have your coat. I can run and grab it now. I'll be quick?"

"Oh sure. Yeah, that'd be great. No rush."

She disappeared toward her dorm and came back less than a minute later, holding my denim jacket. She offered it to me with a smile. "Thank you so much. I'm really sorry about the other night. I was so drunk and I don't remember getting home. My RA told me it was Cobey and his friend that got me home. I don't normally drink, and rest assured, I'm not drinking again any time soon. I tried to find you on social media . . ."

"Oh, I'm not really on social media," I said with a shrug. "Well, apparently I'm all over social media, but not by choice."

She gave me a sad smile, then just kinda stood there.

Was I supposed to say something? Be sociable?

God.

"Did you wanna sit down?" I asked, afraid she'd laugh at me and say no. And also a bit afraid she'd say yes.

Jayda smiled. "Are you sure? I'm not interrupting?"

I showed her the cover of my data analytics textbook. "You'd be doing me a favor."

She laughed and sat down. "I think you're actually in my analytics class."

I stared. "I am?"

She nodded. "I've seen you around."

"Oh, I'm sorry. I keep my head down a lot. I'm not being rude or anything. I'm just not that good with people, sorry. I am actually trying to be better. At the whole peopling thing."

I took a breath and tried to rein in the nerves.

Jayda met my eyes. "I'm not good with people either. As you saw the other night. I thought I'd go out, have a few drinks to meet people, but then it got out of hand. I was trying to be someone I'm not, and that guy kept giving me more and wouldn't let me leave . . ." She made a face. "He's a jerk, and I should have known better."

"No, he's a jerk and you did the right thing by involving Cobey."

She smiled. "He's a good guy."

"He is." I tried not to smile too big at the mere mention of his name.

"I've seen all the social media photos and comments. I'm sorry you have to deal with that."

I sighed, my smile fading. "I don't care about any of that." She gave me a similar look as Cobey when I'd said that. "I mean it. I'm not on social media."

"I know. I tried to find you to message you about your jacket."

I chuckled. "Sorry about that."

"As it turns out, no one can find you on social media. All those photos of you and Cobey, you're not tagged in any of them because you don't exist online."

That made me smile. "So maybe it's a good thing?"

"Oh, believe me, it's a good thing."

We were quiet for a few moments. Then she said, "You really don't have any social media at all?"

I shook my head and pulled out my phone like it was all the proof I needed. "My phone could be in a museum." Then I shrugged. "And I'm lacking on the social aspect of the whole social media concept. I don't have many friends. Which makes it really awkward."

"I don't have many either. I'm twenty-one. I was an au pair in England for two years right after high school because my parents thought traveling would be good for me. Which it was, but now in college, I'm two years behind all my old friends. Kinda got left behind. It hasn't been easy."

I smiled at her. "It's really not easy. Making friends is hard."

"So hard. When you're little, it's so easy. You just had to say hello and smile, give them a sticker, and presto! A new best friend. But now? It's a minefield and people already have established circles."

"Mine's more of a triangle."

She laughed. "Same."

I sighed. "It is hard. Especially when you don't have the coolest clothes or newest tech and you're not cool."

"So true. Or if you don't have the Instagram aesthetic." She rolled her eyes. "People who only care about that aren't real friends."

"True. But I'm trying to get better at not keeping my head down all the time. I'm even supposed to be going to a party tonight." I made a face. "Though it's probably not a party by college fraternity definition. More of a Dungeons and Dragons thing probably."

"Ooh, I love Dungeons and Dragons," Jayda said.

"You do?"

"Yes! I used to play all the time."

"That's cool. I'll have to introduce you to my friend Rafe." Then something occurred to me. "Or you could come with me tonight so I'm not really lame, turning up by myself. Is it weird that I just asked you to do that? God, it's probably weird. It's only a five-minute walk away, apparently, and if it's terrible, we can leave together. My social battery has a short depletion rate, so it won't be a late one."

Jayda smiled. "I'd like that. And it's not weird. It's like the equivalent of giving me a sticker in elementary school."

"Awesome. It starts at like eight. And I want to be back before Cobey gets home." I cringed. "Sorry. I don't mean to talk about him. It's just that he said this game was kind of important and I want to hear all about it."

"I'm surprised you're not there watching."

I sighed. "He offered to get me a lift, and I probably should have gone." Even if it was with his parents. Although the idea of spending hours with his parents when he wasn't there was horrifying. "I don't have the money for tickets or buses, but I kinda wish I could have watched him."

"You can watch it on TV."

I stared at her. "I can?"

She laughed. "Sure. We can go down to Shenanigans if you want. They'll have it on the big screen."

"Oh." I tried not to let my disappointment show. I hated that it always came down to this. The story of my life. "I, uh, I don't have any money. Well, I have some money, but my budget is tight—"

"It's absolutely my treat. We'll get a plate of fries and two sodas and watch the game."

I wanted to protest, but . . .

"You want to watch your boyfriend play?"

It was so weird hearing someone else call him that, and I'm sure I turned beet red. "I would, yes."

She jumped up. "Then come on. It's probably already started."

So I went to Shenanigans with Jayda and we found a booth at the back. The bar was kinda packed and very loud, all attention on the big screen.

And sure enough, there on actual television like it was an NFL game were some very familiar purple jerseys. "Oh my god," I said, stunned. "That's us."

Jayda laughed. "It is."

Something happened in the game and almost everyone stood

up and hollered. From the cheers for Peyton, I assumed our quarterback did something great. But then play changed and our defense took the field.

I had to crane my neck to see past the guy in front who stood up. My heart was in my throat, my nerves were as bad as if I were in the stadium. But then I saw it.

The number 33.

"There he is," I said, grinning like a fool. Cobey was on television! Like an actual football star.

Wait.

Was he actually a real-life football star?

I mean, everyone knew him. Everyone loved him. I knew that much. But was he a sports star?

I knew in my head that college games were a big deal. But to see it, to see our team on TV, to see Cobey playing football on TV . . .

Holy shit.

*My boyfriend's playing football on TV.*

They did the scrimmage line thing, and UCLA passed the ball back, and as their guy went to throw it, a huge blur of purple and gold ran across the field and took him out.

Of course it was the number 33.

Cheers and applause went up in the bar, and a few people called out things like, "Yeah, Cobey!" and "The Green machine," and I couldn't help but laugh.

It was ridiculous how exciting it was.

Cobey was playing football on TV. My boyfriend.

*My boyfriend.*

Jayda laughed at me, nudging me with her elbow, and I couldn't help it. I was grinning like a fool.

Then someone on the UCLA team made a break down the line and Cobey chased after them, taking them out of the field of play. The crowd in the bar went crazy; the roaring on the TV went wild too.

Going into the final quarter, the Kings were in front by eight.

Jayda and I had barely touched our sodas and fries, too enthralled with the game. The whole crowd was into it and it was exciting. Addictive.

All those years I'd never understood people's obsession with the game.

Well, I understood it now.

I wasn't as interested in the game when our offensive team was on, admittedly. My very biased interest was in the defense. We scored again via an impressive play by Peyton, widening the lead even more. But UCLA wasn't giving up easy. Their guy pitted against Cobey was huge. Bigger than Cobey, hellbent on blocking him, and I had a pit of nervous dread in my belly.

*Don't hurt him. Just don't hurt him.*

"God, I can't even watch," I said, looking through my fingers. "Is he okay?"

Jayda laughed. "He's fine. Watch."

And sure enough, as UCLA set up their line, Cobey was calling shots and pointing. And when they broke, it was Cobey who forced an incompletion. Then he did something called covering and blitzing, and I really had so much to learn. He tackled someone else and smashed that really big guy in another play.

The crowd in the bar was hollering and I was so excited I had to sit on my hands to stop from floundering.

Even the commentators were so hyped. "I think we'll be seeing a lot more of number 33 for the Kings, Cobey Green. Kid's got a very bright future."

"He makes linebacking look easy."

"He just took out their quarterback!"

The Kings won and my nerves didn't settle down until the game was well and truly over.

"You okay?" Jayda asked me.

I nodded. "I think so? God, I think I have an ulcer."

Her eyes glanced past me and she spoke in a whisper. "Well, I won't tell you that people might have realized you're here."

What?

"Me? Why would anyone care about me?"

"Uh, because there are a whole bunch of photographs of you kissing one of the star players they just watched on TV."

"Oh." I grimaced. "Right."

Jayda frowned. "Wanna go?"

I nodded, and we quickly grabbed our things and left. And yeah, people watched us. One person even said, "Hey, Vincent." I think they were in my analytics class but I'd never spoken to them before.

It was awkward, and to be honest, a little overwhelming. And of course Gavin was at the bar, sneering at both of us as we made our way outside.

The fresh salt air was a relief, the sunset a pretty orange, and we were quiet for half the walk back. "Well, that was fun," I said. "Until the leaving part."

"It was fun," Jayda said. "You still going to that party tonight?"

"Oh shit. I kinda forgot about it." I sighed. "And honestly, it's the last thing I feel like doing but I told Rafe I'd be there. You don't have to come if you'd rather not."

We stopped outside her dorm. "Can I be honest with you, Vincent?"

Oh great. Was I about to be dumped by a brand-new friend? Did friends do that?

*Here it comes. The gentle let down.*

"Yes. Of course," I said, trying to make it less awkward. "I know I'm not that much of a conversationalist."

"What? Oh my god, are you kidding? Vincent, that's what I wanted to say. I *do* want to go tonight. I need to meet new people as well, and I've enjoyed hanging out with you this afternoon."

"Oh. I just assumed when you asked if you could be honest . . ."

She shook her head, smiling. "No, I was going to say it's actually kinda great to hang out with someone who's smart and not caught up on all that social media bullshit. And, for the super honest part, it's nice to have a guy friend who doesn't expect . . . anything from me."

"Expect anything? I don't . . ." Then it dawned on me what she meant. "Oh. Yes, rest assured I don't expect that. Please don't be offended. I'm very gay."

She laughed, a little embarrassed. "No offense taken at all, believe me." She took out her phone and checked the time. "Okay, I'll meet you back here at eight."

We exchanged numbers and I went back up to my room. I flopped down on my bed and I realized I was smiling.

I'd made a new friend today.

And it wasn't lost on me that I'd told her, very bluntly, that I was gay. I'd said the words so easily. I barely recognized this new me. This version of me that I'd always wanted to be.

Still smiling, I looked across at Cobey's bed. At the posters on the wall, the photographs. I couldn't wait for Cobey to get back tonight. I was giddy with the mere thought of seeing him. Butter-flies fluttered in my belly; my heart beat staccato.

Words kept echoing through my mind, ridiculously and prob-ably far too prematurely.

*You love him. You're so in love with him.*

I could admit it to myself. No way was I saying it to him anytime soon. I'd never really known love. Not from anyone, not even my father. So maybe I was mistaking what my heart was trying to say.

Maybe it was infatuation or lust. My first physical relationship. So yes, lust made sense and my body certainly agreed. But I was scared of falling too hard, too fast, like I hadn't already fallen. I was so out of my depth; if my feelings were a pool, I was well and truly underwater.

*Stop overthinking it, Vincent.*

*Stop overthinking it.*

With a sigh, I rolled off the bed, changed my shirt, and fresh-ened up a bit, then went to grab a bite to eat before meeting Jayda.

She came down wearing jeans, yellow Chuck Taylors, and a Sailor Moon shirt. And a huge grin.

"You look great," I said. It was a far cry from the outfit she'd been wearing the other night at the bar.

She did a twirl. "This is me," she said. "The real me. I don't want to try to fit into other people's idea of me anymore."

My grin matched hers. "Well, confidence looks good on you."

"Thank you," she replied. "Are you ready?"

"Not at all," I said. "I've never actually been to a party before. I have no idea what to expect, and I don't know how many people will be there. It's highly unlikely I'll know anyone, apart from Rafe."

"You'll be fine," she said as we began walking. "I won't know anyone apart from you, so we can be socially awkward together."

"Promise me we won't be there for long."

"I promise."

Rafe lived in a shared house with four other people, all students at FU. He opened the door, clearly surprised to see me. "Oh wow, you actually came!"

I made introductions that went something like, "Hey Jayda, nice to meet you, oh my god, I love your shirt," and then we were taken around and introduced. There were about twenty people, dotted in small groups throughout the house. A few faces I recognized from the tutor group, but everyone smiled at us and said hello.

There was music, and people laughed and chatted. There were some bags of chips and plenty of sodas.

It was nowhere near as terrible as I thought it would be.

Until one girl asked me the dreaded question . . . "Oh, I knew I recognized you. You're Cobey Green's boyfriend, right? I've seen all the pics on Insta."

Great.

I swear the music stopped playing and people turned, waiting for me to answer. It was possible that over-dramatization was entirely in my head, but it surely felt real.

*Boyfriend. You're about to admit it publicly for the first time in your entire life. Take a breath.*

"Uh, yes." I ignored the heat in my cheeks. "I am. He is . . . we are."

"Oh, he's just so sweet," she replied. "He was in my media class last year."

"Yeah, he's kinda great." I was certain the temperature of my face could be measured in Kelvin. But thankfully she didn't press for information or ask anything personal. Everyone was just kinda . . . nice.

Jayda and I stayed for about another hour. She seemed to know when I'd reached my limit, and we said goodbye to Rafe and headed home.

"Soooo?" she asked. "How was it?"

"It wasn't terrible," I said. "I actually had a good time."

"Oh my god, same! And I met two girls in my chem class who were pretty cool. They liked my shirt. They told me to come find them before class sometime, so I'm stoked. Now I won't be such a loser."

"Well, you still have to be friends with me, so don't get too popular."

She bumped her hip to mine and laughed. "Says the guy who's dating the most popular guy in our whole year."

"I still can't believe it, you know. That he even likes me at all. As if I've woken up in some strange dream. It's all very surreal."

"I've seen the photos online, Vincent. How he looks at you."

"Hm. Maybe I should get Instagram or TikTok." Though honestly, I couldn't think of anything worse. "Because I haven't seen them. I mean, I don't care about the comments or the lies or whatever. But maybe seeing the photos couldn't hurt."

"I can send you screenshots of them."

"You would? Because I don't have any."

"Then I'll send you them all. But only the ones where you look amazing."

I sighed happily. "You know, having a friend is actually pretty cool."

She laughed and skipped up the steps to her dorm, thanking me again for a great day and making promises to talk again soon. I went up to my room, happy. It had been a great day but I was grateful to change into my sweat pants and climb into bed for some peace and quiet.

I missed Cobey.

Which was stupid. And needy. And I would honestly roll my eyes at myself if the missing-him part didn't feel so real.

Then my phone rang . . . no, not a call. A FaceTime. Of course it was Cobey.

The screen came on, lagging a little, and it took me a second to recognize that he was at Shenanigans. The bar was packed and pumping. He moved to a darker, quieter part. "Hey, we just got in. We were late getting back," he said.

"I watched your game. On TV. You were amazing today."

"You watched?"

"Of course I did. I wished I was there."

He looked at the screen, his head tilted. "Hey, uh, where are you?"

I lifted my phone so he could see the Mary-Jesus-Adam-Driver poster. "I'm in your bed. I missed you, which is stupid, I know. But I figured you'd be with your friends for a while."

He scrubbed his hand over his face and someone close by said something. "Jesus, Vee. You can't be saying shit like that to me."

"I'm sorry—"

He brought his phone in close so all I could see was half his face. "Don't apologize," he whispered. "And don't get out of my bed. I'll be there in five minutes."

## COBEY

Vincent looked all warm and cozy, he said he missed me, and he was in my bed. There was no way I wasn't going to him. But of course the guys weren't gonna let me go without some jokes first.

"You bailing on us so soon?" Peyton said.

"You are so whipped," Jared added.

I ignored that. "I've been with you guys all day and had to listen to your sorry asses sing on the bus for the last however fucking long," I joked. "Plus, my back's killing me." I grimaced and pretended to hold my lower back. "From carrying you guys all game."

That earned me some laughs and one or two shoves. "And you got a better offer," Nate said with a wink and a raised beer bottle. "You are so fucking whipped, Green."

I clapped his shoulder, none too gently. "I got a *much* better offer. I will see you dickheads tomorrow."

They jeered me as I left, but I didn't care.

I hightailed it back to the dorm, took the stairs two at a time, and fumbled to unlock the door. "Dammit, Vee, I shoulda asked you to unlock it."

He laughed as I almost fell inside. And there he was, still in my bed, leaning against the headboard reading a book, with his floppy hair and glasses. The only light was the reading light and the whole room was soft, and he looked so damned sexy, it stopped me where I stood.

My heart banged, my blood was hot, and my insides were all swoopy.

"Christ, Vee."

He closed the book. "What?"

"You're so fucking hot right now. Look at you."

And then he had to blush and make it even worse.

Or better.

So much better.

I pulled off my jacket and threw it on my desk, then toed out of my shoes. I crawled up the bed, watching Vincent's face as he watched me. The dark eyes, the smile, the lip bite.

Christ.

Still on my hands and knees, our noses just an inch apart, I took his hips and pulled him down the bed. He yelped out a laugh before I laid on top of him and kissed him.

He deepened the kiss as his hands found my hair, my neck, my shoulders, my face. His legs spread to accommodate me.

I fit so good.

There was still a blanket between us but I was in no hurry. I wanted to enjoy this. Our kisses became slow, like Vincent wanted to enjoy it too.

"You missed me today?" I asked, kissing down to his ear.

"I did." He gasped when I kissed that spot under his ear. "Is that crazy?"

"No. Because I missed you too."

"I should have gone to watch your game. I'm sorry I didn't."

I nudged his nose to mine and kissed him again. "But you watched it?"

He nodded. "I went with Jayda, to the bar. We got fries and soda but I was too nervous watching you. I was a nervous wreck."

I pulled back a little. "Wait up. You went to Shenanigans. With Jayda."

He chuckled, nodding. "She gave me back my jacket, and we got talking. She's actually really nice. I asked her to go to Rafe's party with me."

I pulled back some more. "You went to the party as well?"

He laughed. "I made a new friend. I went to a bar to watch football on a big screen, and then I went to a party. All in one day."

I cracked up laughing and kissed him, both of us smiling. "That's a big day for you."

"Oh, and let's not forget that I watched you play football on TV like some huge NFL player. It was crazy! I had no idea they did that. Cobey, you should have seen the crowd at the bar cheering for you. And the commentators on TV? They loved you. It was amazing, and I was so proud. Because it was you! Cobey, they were saying you've got a bright future. Do you know how big that is?"

I laughed. "Uh, yeah." He was so stinking cute, I couldn't stand it.

"But they kept calling you Mike, so you really should have someone tell them that's not your name."

I laughed really fucking loud, rolled us onto our sides, put my hand to his face, and brushed my lips to his. "Vincent, don't ever change."

He was confused, clearly. "Is Mike a football thing?"

I nodded. "Yeah."

"Oh." He deflated a little. "I need to learn more. And I want to go to your next game. All of them. If my nerves can hold out."

"I'd like that. Next game's a home game. I'll get you a pass. Then maybe you could come back to the bar with me? If you can go with Jayda . . ."

"You want me there?"

I met his eyes and nodded. "Everyone has their girlfriends or boyfriends there. But only if you'd be comfortable with that."

Panic flashed in his eyes and he swallowed hard but gave a nod. "For you. I'd do that for you."

I kissed him again, and this time it was leading somewhere. He unbuttoned my shirt, and when I got off the bed to pull off my pants, he took off his sweatpants and held up the covers for me.

Lying with him, our bodies tangled up, felt so good. Better than good.

It felt right.

We made out, slow and deep and so amazing, and ended up giving lazy mutual hand jobs. And after we'd cleaned up, we fell asleep in my bed, wrapped around each other. His body fit to mine like he was made just for me. Perfect in every way.

Nate's words came back to me as I drifted off.

*You're so fucking whipped.*

Yes, yes I was.

And it was incredible. I fell asleep smiling. Woke up like it too.

VINCENT and I had a busy week. Aside from a lot of making out and mutual orgasms, we'd had sex one more time. We'd spooned and I'd taken him from behind. It was better for him on our sides that way and he'd enjoyed it a lot more.

He also had his tutoring sessions like usual, and I had all my training and gym sessions, but he still insisted on making me do our agreed calculus lessons.

He was good at what he did. His knowledge of all things math was perfect.

Mine, not so much.

He made it look so easy, but I just couldn't get my head around it. "I don't even know what implicit differentiation means," I whined. It was late on Thursday and I'd gone to the gym *and* been to training, and I was totally wiped. We were sitting on his bed and I would have rather done anything else. "Can't we just make out instead?

"You have a test in two weeks," he said. "And this weekend is busy with the home game, and the weekend after that you're in Palm Springs." He sighed. "But it's late and you're tired. I'm sorry."

I closed my book and shoved it aside. "It's not your fault. I just don't understand it. It might as well be some foreign language. Hell, it *is* a foreign language. I'm gonna fail it for sure."

He frowned and closed his laptop before crawling over to straddle me. He slung his arms around my neck and kissed me. "You're not going to fail."

My hands went to his hips and he rocked back and forth, grinding on me. "I like this much better," I murmured.

He moaned. "Same. God, Cobey. I want you . . . like this . . ."

I held him still and he locked eyes with me. "You want me inside you like this?"

He nodded quickly. Embarrassed, aroused.

It took some time, getting naked, getting the condom and lube, getting him ready for me. But I sat on his bed, leaning against the headboard, and he straddled me, slowly impaling himself on my cock.

He was so tight, so hot. So in control. So fucking sexy.

He set the pace, every movement, every sound he made, every gasp and groan. He was in complete control. I wanted to grip his hips and drive up into him, and it took every ounce of self-control I had not to.

He was so beautiful, and he felt so damn good.

When I was fully seated inside him, his head lolled back and he groaned out a real guttural sound. His cock was semi-hard, so I stroked him and he cried out. His eyes rolled back and his body jerked, sending jolts of pleasure through me.

Then he began to slide up and down, real slow. Torturously slow. I was completely at his mercy.

I'd never felt a pleasure like it.

"Vincent, you're gonna make me come," I rasped.

His head snapped forward and he grunted as he kissed me. He held onto me, leaning in so his cock now slid between our bodies. And he rocked back and forth until I couldn't hold back anymore.

I held him, tight as I dared, as my orgasm hit me. I flexed up into him, pulsing as I came. "Fuck, Vincent. God, yes."

He gasped, riding it out, his head lolled back. His precome smeared between us, on my belly and chest, and he pumped his cock until he spilled his load over his hand, over me. He writhed and groaned, and I held his hips as he rode out the waves of his orgasm.

It was so fucking hot.

He slumped onto me, spent and boneless. And afterwards, he

was so sleepy, so happy. I wrapped him up in my arms and the blankets and I almost told him I loved him.

I almost said it.

I almost said those three words. I wanted to. I wanted him to know, but I just couldn't bring myself to say it.

I held him extra tight and kissed the side of his head instead.

ON THE SATURDAY before the game, I was running late. And I'd held off giving Vincent the tickets to the game for a very good reason. I'd called him to find out where he was and I found him and Jayda sitting at a picnic table in the quad.

"Okay, so here are the game tickets," I said, handing over an envelope. I was puffing from running. Coach was going to kill me.

Vincent looked at the envelope, then up to me. "Tickets? As in plural?"

"Yep. One for you, one for Jayda." They'd been hanging out a bit, which was kind of cute.

"Oh?" she said, smiling brightly. "Thank you so much!"

*Here goes nothing.*

I took a step back. "And there's two for my parents. I told them to meet you here. Mom was bringing a bag of stuff from home for me. If you could just throw it on my bed, that'd be great. Well, maybe don't throw it. You know what I mean." He was looking kinda horrified, so I took another step back. "Then they'll go with you to the stadium. They're excited to meet you, properly this time."

His mouth fell open.

I took another step back. "I sent them a photo to remind them of what you look like so they know who to look for. I really gotta go. I'm late as it is. Coach is gonna kick my ass."

Vincent stood there, looking all kinds of lost and horrified. "Cobey . . ."

I was just going to turn and run, but the fear on his face stopped me. I walked back to him and took his face in my hands. "Cobey," he whispered. "How can I meet your parents? My own father doesn't even like me."

*Oh baby, no.*

I pressed my forehead to his, feeling bad for dumping this surprise on him. "They are going to love you," I said. "Because I do." And then I kissed him.

Onlookers clapped. Someone whistled.

Vincent blushed, dropping his head down. So I lifted his chin. "I really do have to go. Coach is gonna kill me. I'll see you at Shenanigans after the game."

He was a little teary, but he was smiling and he nodded. "Okay. Kick ass today."

I was grinning as I ran out, and I was still grinning when I ran into the locker room. The entire coaching team was there. Coach took one look at me and at my still-grinning face. "The hell have you been?"

"Just getting my game on, Coach."

He muttered something to himself before looking me up and down. "You gonna bring it today, Green?"

"All game long, Coach."

"Good." I thought for a second he was gonna tell me to stop smiling but he shook his head as he walked away, mumbling something else I couldn't hear.

I turned to find a few teammates looking at me. Nate shook his head. "Fucking whipped."

# TWELVE

## VINCENT

"JESUS CHRIST," I said, still trying to catch my breath. "He said . . . he told me . . . he . . ."

"I heard." Jayda rubbed my arm. "Are you okay?"

"I think so?" I sounded as if I'd ingested an entire helium balloon. It would explain the tightness in my chest. "And I'm meeting his parents."

"I know."

"Today. Any minute now. With no warning. And what photo did he send them?"

She nodded. "Vincent, you'll be fine. I'll be with you."

"I'm going to kill him, you know."

She looked over my shoulder and made a face. "Okay, so there's no more time for freaking out because there's an older couple who just walked in and the guy is a forty-year-old double for Cobey. It has to be them. They're looking kind of lost."

I turned around and, sure enough, it was his parents. I'd seen them for half a second the day Cobey moved in. I stood up at the same time his mom spotted me. She smiled and I did some awkward hand-wave thing. She grabbed her husband's arm and they came toward us.

Oh god.

*Don't freak out, don't freak out.*

"Oh, Vincent, it's so nice to meet you again," his mom said, warmly. I got the impression she wanted to hug me but restrained herself.

"Mrs. Green, Mr. Green," I replied. "This is my friend Jayda. She's coming to the game with us."

"Ooh, how lovely," Mrs. Green said.

"Please, call us Sheree and Chris," Mr. Green said. He really did look like an older version of Cobey. Same height, same blue eyes. He was carrying a backpack and he held it out for me. But there was no way I was calling them by their given names. "I was told I had to give this to you."

"Oh, right. I'll just run it upstairs," I said. "Won't be a minute." I gave an apologetic glance at Jayda and raced the bag up to our room. I placed it on Cobey's bed, and as I turned around, I spotted something slung over his desk chair.

A certain hoodie.

A certain FU Kings hoodie with Green 33 on the back . . .

*Should I?*

*Shouldn't I?*

It was, apparently, something only couples did. And we were officially boyfriends now. And earlier he said the L word to me. Not "I love you" directly, but close enough.

*"My parents will love you. Because I do."*

It made me stupidly giddy. He said that to me! He said those words. He loved me. Cobey Green loved me.

So I took the hoodie. It was too warm for it right then, so I tied it around my waist and went back downstairs. Jayda and Mrs. Green were laughing, so it seemed they got along okay. I took the tickets out and handed two over to Mr. Green. "Cobey gave me these."

"Excellent, thank you."

Before I could say anything else, Mrs. Green grabbed my arm and we began walking out. "We better get on our way," she said. "Now, tell me about you, Vincent. Cobey tells me you're the smartest person he's ever met."

"Oh—"

"And he tells me you're helping him with calculus."

"Well, I—"

"And he said you've been dating for a little while now."

I almost tripped over my feet, but thankfully I didn't fall.

"Jeez, Sheree. Leave the kid alone," Mr. Green said with a smile. "You wanted him to tell you all about himself but don't give him a chance to speak."

She told him to shush, and Jayda laughed.

I was trying not to die of embarrassment. "Ah, I don't know everyone that Cobey's ever met so I can't say if I'm the smartest, but statistically speaking, I might be in the top two percent. And yes, I'm trying to help him with calculus. I'm sure he can do it, but he gets frustrated with it so easily. And yes, we are dating . . ." My face went a color to rival Schrödinger's red.

She thankfully chose not to comment on the heat radiating out of my face. "Tell me about your parents," she said, still holding onto my arm.

"Oh, uh." Shit. "Well, my mother left when I was very young. I don't remember her."

Mrs. Green frowned. "Oh no, I'm sorry. So it was just you and your dad?"

I grimaced. "Well, yes and no. Sometimes it was. Most of the time it was just me."

"Oh my word," she said, tightening her hold on my arm. She didn't say anything for a bit. "You must be tenacious and driven because here you are at a great college." She winked. "With a great boyfriend."

Mr. Green groaned. "Sheree, honey. Didn't Cobey also ask you to not interrogate him?"

"I'm not interrogating him."

"Honey, you could get a job at the CIA."

Mrs. Green shushed him again. Jayda laughed and I found myself smiling.

I realized that while Cobey looked like his dad, he really was like his mom. Just open honesty, blunt and open-hearted. And maybe with his dad's sense of humor.

We found our seats in the stadium and Mrs. Green suggested she and Jayda go for some snacks, leaving me and Mr. Green alone.

Great.

"So," he began. I held my breath, fully expecting the third degree about dating his son, or maybe about being gay, or . . . oh my god, please not about safe sex . . . "Cobey said you're studying math and tech science."

I exhaled, pure relief. "Yes, a double major. I want to get into data science. That's the plan, anyway."

"Data science," he said, nodding thoughtfully. "Interesting choice."

"I like numbers. Well, actually, it's more that I understand math and correlating data. And it's a developing industry, especially in tech. I'd prefer a career that adapts to changes as it grows and I like learning new things." I sighed. "And it pays well."

He smiled now. "You know, what you said about Cobey earlier. About him getting frustrated with calculus . . ."

"Yeah?"

"The thing with Cobey is, he's good at most things he does. Any sport he tried, he'd ace it on day one. Pick up a baseball bat and hit nothing but home runs. Put him on a track and he'd win all damn day. Basketball, wrestling, you name it. He was good without even trying. And if he wasn't good at it, he wouldn't be there on day two. Couldn't keep him interested. See, the thing with subjects like calculus is that he thinks he's lost before he starts. He convinces himself he'll never get it and his brain switches off."

This sounded very much like Cobey.

"But the thing is, he uses math out there"—he gestured to the football field—"and he doesn't even realize it. Sure, he can tell you all about pass completion percentages, yards per game, touchdown to interception ratio. Every kid out there can. But to Cobey, that's football, not math. There's calculus in football, and he knows it without knowing he knows it. If that makes sense."

I looked out to the field, to the yard lines. Calculus in football . . .

Mr. Green chuckled. "You never picked up on the math?"

I met his gaze. "Uh, to be frank, Mr. Green, I'd never watched a game of football before I met Cobey."

He stared. "Not one?"

"Not a single minute." I shrugged. "I didn't watch much TV as a kid. I basically grew up in a public library, and in high school I avoided all the jocks because, hello, nerdy gay boy here at Millside High School."

He winced. "Sorry."

I shrugged. "And then Cobey got me a ticket to my very first game a few weeks ago, and honestly, I didn't even pay attention to anything but the tight uniforms."

He laughed, and I wasn't even embarrassed.

"And the second game wasn't much better. I spent the entire time watching Cobey annihilate the opposition, trying to align the monster defenseman Cobey on the field to the sweet and funny Cobey I know." I shook my head. "And again, with the uniform, I mean, how does he even get into that thing?"

Mr. Green laughed again and he patted my leg. "Okay, so maybe today while the offense is on, you can see the math behind the game. Then when he's on, you can admire the uniform."

I wasn't sure how that wasn't awkward at all. But it was as casual as discussing the weather.

Except it was Cobey's father.

Oh boy.

I had no idea how this was my life.

Mrs. Green and Jayda came back, arms full of drinks and hotdogs, and soon enough the game began.

The crowd roared when the Kings took the field, and for a petite woman, Mrs. Green sure could holler when Cobey ran out. Not that I could judge because I even clapped and cheered, even though my nerves were just about frazzled raw.

Every time he was out there, I had to watch through my fingers. I felt every hit, every charge, every tackle, and by the second quarter, I felt like I'd been the one out on the field.

Mr. Green must have taken some pity on me because at half-time and into the third quarter, he began pointing things out.

Like a player's breakaway speed, noting the rates of change. Arc lengths of ball trajectories, angle optimizations, defense formations, and momentum . . .

And I began to see his point.

How had I not noticed this before?

I'd been trying to tutor Cobey in calculus using calculus. What I should have been doing was tutoring him in calculus using football.

I felt like a fool. Foolish for not understanding how the student needed to learn.

The Kings won the game, the heroes of the day were the quarterback and the wide receiver. But the middle linebacker had an outstanding game too. I might have been biased, but Cobey was on fire. I could even hear him yelling, telling his defense team what to do, where to be. He read that game like a newspaper. Their offense never stood a chance.

He was amazing.

The whole stadium was on their feet as the boys celebrated their win. They did their huddle thing, chest bumps, and helmet slaps, and when it died down a little, Cobey scanned the crowd.

His mom and dad waved their arms, and I could see it on Cobey's face when he saw them. And then, when he saw me.

His parents had to have seen it too.

Jayda nudged me, and when Cobey left the field, she grabbed my arm and did a little jumpy dance. "This is so exciting!"

I fell back in my seat, my hand to my heart. "I think I need to invest in some Xanax. Not sure my heart can take this."

Mr. Green gave my shoulder a gentle shake. "You'll get used to it. Now let's go eat."

Yep. Definitely Cobey's dad.

## COBEY

We kicked ass. No two ways about it. But I was excited to get back to the bar. My folks would be there, sure. But Vincent was going to be there too.

Man, seeing him in the crowd standing right next to my dad, both of them smiling at me . . . well, it felt good. It felt right. Like something settled in my bones right then and there.

I'd also told him I loved him today.

I was on a fucking high.

The bar was packed, the crowd and music were pumping, and they began to cheer as we walked in. It was a crazy rush, being applauded like that. There were so many people, I couldn't see my parents yet.

But Bumbles found his girlfriend and kissed her, and Travone found his girl and scooped her up in a hug. And it was probably silly, and god knows I'd never admit to anyone, but that's what I wanted. I wanted to be able to walk into the bar after a game and see my person.

I wanted to share my win with my someone-special.

Vincent.

I thought I caught a glimpse of my dad through the crowd and I had to look twice . . . The guy standing at their table had his back to me and all I could see was the writing on his hoodie.

# GREEN
## 33

Vincent was wearing my hoodie. With my name and number on it. He was wearing my name, telling every single person in that bar that he was mine.

I made my way through the crowd. People tried to get out of my way, but it was packed and others wanted to say hi. A smiling Jayda tapped Vincent's arm and he turned around just in time for me to pull him close, slide my hand along his jaw, and kiss him.

The whole bar cheered.

Someone wolf-whistled, which may or may not have been my mom.

I pulled back and laughed as Vincent's cheeks went red. Maybe it was the neon lights, but I knew how he blushed and it looked deliciously familiar.

"I'm so happy you're here," I told him, then tucked him in under my arm as I reached over to greet my parents.

It was such a great night.

We talked, we laughed, my arm around his shoulder in front of my parents, in front of all my teammates, in front of all of FU. There would be photos online already, I had no doubt.

But I'd never apologized for being queer and I certainly wasn't about to start now. As long as Vincent was okay with it—and he was—then I would proudly have him at my side.

When Mom and Dad left, they hugged me and then they hugged Vincent, and Mom even hugged a surprised Jayda. By then, most of the guys on my team who couldn't drink had already gone home, and the thinned-out crowd was down to the guys who'd all had a few beers and bourbons.

I was ready to leave.

"You good to go?" I asked Vincent.

"Oh. Did you not want to stay and watch Jared sing that song from *Frozen*?"

I snorted. "No, I do not." Then I leaned in and whispered in his ear. "I'd rather be in our room."

"Oh."

"For goodness' sake, you two," Jayda said, standing up. "Come on. You can walk this third wheel home."

I said goodbye to the guys, slung my arm around Vincent's shoulder, and we left.

We got Jayda to the steps of her dorm, where she thanked us for a great day, did a twirl in her Power Ranger shirt, and went inside.

Vincent laughed, put his arm around my waist, and we headed toward our dorm. "So," he said. "Your parents are great."

"They are."

"Your mom had three pink gins. Your dad said she doesn't normally drink very often."

"That explains the hugging."

Vincent laughed.

"Can we talk about you wearing this hoodie to the bar tonight?"

He stopped walking and looked up at me, his eyes wide. "Was it wrong? I just . . . I remembered you saying it was what boyfriends or girlfriends did and so—"

I pulled him against me, our hips flush. "It was fucking hot. Seeing you in the bar wearing my name and my number like that. Hottest thing you coulda done. Quite the power play, Vee."

"A power what?"

I laughed. "A boss move. You wore that like you were telling everyone, 'Yeah, he's mine. Whatcha gonna do about it?' and that's hot as fuck."

"Oh, I uh . . ."

I lifted his chin and kissed him. "Hot as fuck."

He swallowed hard and whispered, "I think we should go to our room."

WITH A KISS TO HIS TEMPLE, I left Vincent in my bed, wrung out and fast asleep. I had some team stuff to do, even though leaving him was the last thing I wanted. We'd spent hours in bed last night, making out, making love. There wasn't one inch of that man's body I wasn't familiar with.

But yeah, I had stuff to do, and he would probably need to sleep for a while yet. I'd worked him over last night pretty hard. Not that he was complaining. Hell no. He fucking loved it. Begged for it.

God, how he'd begged for it . . .

Great.

Now I was gonna walk into a room full of my teammates and coaching team with a hard-on.

It wasn't easy to concentrate on our post-game analogy. I had to make myself not think about Vincent, about his body, the way he laughs, the way he groans. I had to *make* myself focus. Time dragged, and by the time we were done, I was hungry and tired, and all I wanted to do was grab some tacos and maybe take an afternoon nap.

When I got back, Vincent was sitting at his desk with his laptop and a notepad, pen in hand. That wasn't too surprising. He often was. But this time he had football on his screen. He hit Pause when I came in, looked up at me, and grinned. "Hey, you."

I leaned down and kissed him. "What are you watching?"

"Replays of your last televised games."

I laughed in disbelief. "Why?"

He showed me his notepad, clearly excited. "Your dad said something to me yesterday, and it made a lot of sense."

"My dad . . ."

"Yes. How calculus correlates to football. It's actually really fascinating." Then he pointed back to the screen, to me holding the ball at the 20-yard line. "See here, at this point of axis."

I put my hand up like I was stopping traffic. I was smiling because he was so damn cute, but calculus? "Babe."

He blinked and dropped his hand to his lap. "Babe? Is that a thing we're doing now?"

I laughed and threw myself on my bed, pulling my pillow under my head. "Please, no calculus. I am beat. My brain is fried, my body is sore. I'm hungry and tired. I want tacos and maybe even a nap."

He walked over to me, frowning. "Are you okay? What can I do?" He sat down and took my hand. "Are you sore from playing yesterday? You made a lot of hits. Is there something I can get for you? I can get you something from the dining hall if you'd like."

I sighed and kissed his hand with smiling lips. "You know what I would really like? If we walked down to get tacos on the pier. That would fix me."

"Okay."

I nodded over to his laptop. "What about your math theory? I didn't mean to interrupt you."

"Don't worry. I'll tell you all about it. We'll be going over it a lot before now and your exam."

I groaned. "But babe . . ."

He laughed. "Don't weaponize sweet talk, mister. At this moment, your calculus exam is the most important thing. Because if you fail it, there's no football, and if you have to leave college, there's no us. So yes, calculus. Every day until you get it right."

I squeezed his hand. "You're wrong."

He looked stunned. "I'm what?"

I snorted. "You're wrong. I understand that's not something you hear often. Or possibly ever. But you're wrong about there being no us. Even if I wasn't here, there'd still be an us."

He smiled and leaned in for a kiss, but I stopped him. "Unless you wouldn't want me if I didn't play football? I mean, you're watching YouTube videos of it now."

He dug his fingers into my ribs, tickling me. I yelped and tried to wriggle away, laughing, and he jumped up and straddled me, holding my arms down. I could have easily fought him off but it was fun. He looked down at me, trying to be scary but just being cuter. "I only care about football because of you," he said. "If you decided to take up baseball, I'd be correlating calculus to . . . whatever it is baseball players do." I laughed and he leaned down to kiss me. "Whatever career you choose, Cobey," he whispered. "Football or no football."

He let my hands go and I held his waist instead. "As much as I love this position. And as much as I know *you* love this position . . ." I said, and he smiled. "What I really choose right now is tacos."

He laughed and hopped off. "Then let's get you some tacos."

We got enough tacos to feed me and one for him, and found a seat by the beach. He ate his one little taco and sipped his soda, then he eyed me cautiously. Probably because I was shoveling my third taco into my face. "Sorry, I'm just hungry."

He laughed and waved me off. "Don't apologize. You need to eat."

I washed it all down with a drink and held out the tray with two remaining tacos. "Did you want another one?"

"No, I'm fine," he said. His eyes searched mine. "I was thinking about what you said yesterday, that your parents will love me because you do. I don't know if that was just some spur of the moment thing . . ."

I shook my head, my heart suddenly in my throat. I hadn't expected him to bring it up so randomly. "Not a spur of the moment. It's true. As real as I am here right now."

His smile was instant, his cheeks tinted pink. He studied his hands for a few long seconds. "I feel the same about you," he whispered, then let out a long, shaky breath. "Damn, that's not easy to say."

I leaned over and kissed the side of his head. "Thank you."

His eyes met mine, different now. Urgent and sorry, even, and I knew what he was about to say was important. I put the tray of food down and gave him my undivided attention. "You know I had a pretty fucked up childhood."

I nodded.

"There were a lot of things missing from my life. I went without a lot of things."

"Like food. You don't eat enough."

He smiled and kinda shrugged it off. "Yeah, maybe. I never had a lot of food. But I eat every day now, so that's better."

Fucking hell.

"What I didn't have growing up, what was missing the most," he murmured, "was love. I was on my own a lot. I still am. I mean, I have no family. My dad has barely said two words to me in over a year. Even then it was just a grunt. The time before that was when I graduated high school when he told me he was no longer responsible for me."

"Fuck, Vee. I'm sorry."

"It's okay. It's hard to miss something that you never had. You know?"

I didn't know. Because I'd never come close to experiencing that.

"What I'm trying to say," he said, then swallowed hard. "Is that I might not always get it right and I might not always say the right thing. I might not know how to react to some things. It's just because it's all so new to me. But Cobey, if you do love me—"

"I do."

He gave me a teary smile. "Your love is a gift I will never take for granted. Ever. And the feelings I have for you, that you make me feel, mean a lot to me. To have that in my life. To experience that. It's because of you."

I took hold of his face and kissed him, then pulled him into my side, my arm tight around his shoulders. I kissed the side of his head. "It means a lot to me too. And I won't get it right every time either, Vee. It's all kinda new to me too. But we'll be okay, you and me."

He nodded. "You and me."

"Hang on," I said, taking out my phone. I took a selfie of my smile and the top of his head in the crook of my neck. I showed it to him. "Is this okay?"

"What for?"

"My new socials avi."

"Um, sure."

I swapped out the photo of me with a football. "This'll keep the internet busy for a while. Should probably turn off notifications for a day or two."

He sighed. "So glad I don't have any of that."

The truth was, I was kinda glad he didn't have social media as well. Only because people would have bombarded him and tried to find out shit from his past. And also it meant the online trolls couldn't touch him. Not that his phone could probably handle too many apps.

"Oh, that reminds me," I said. *I wasn't sure how he was going to react to this* . . . "You're not allowed to be mad at me."

He sat up straight and looked at me. "Mad?"

"I won't get mad at you for making me do calculus if you don't get mad at me," I tried.

He rolled his eyes. "What is it?"

"It's probably best if I show you."

He glanced down at my phone, more worried now. "What is it?"

"It's nothing bad." I shoveled the two remaining tacos into my mouth like a heathen and tossed the tray into the trash. "Come on, it's in our room."

He eyed me warily the whole way back to our dorm, and when he sat on the edge of his bed, he wiped his palms on his jeans. "I'm not good with surprises, Cobey," he said. "So if you could just put me out of my misery, that'd be great."

"Misery?" I repeated with a laugh. "It's not bad. It's good. I think. I hope. I don't know how you'll react, to be honest." I picked up the backpack my mom had brought yesterday. "I had my mom bring some stuff from home."

He nodded because he knew this. He was the one who put the bag in our room . . .

"It's for you."

He looked at me, then the bag, then back at me. "What's for me?"

"All this."

He made no attempt at taking it. He just stared at me. "What's in it?"

I unzipped it, reached in, and took out the first thing. It was my old phone and I handed it to him. "Now before you say anything, this has been sitting in my desk drawer for a year. My phone is on my dad's contract and I get a new one every two years. I know that sounds bad, and I know I'm privileged and lucky, but there's nothing wrong with this one, and it's about four years newer than yours. You just need to put your sim card in it and you're good to go."

"Cobey," he whispered. He looked horrified.

Shit.

"It just sat in my desk at home," I added quickly. "You might as well use it. I know yours glitches out on you a bit, and this'll get you through college at least."

Then I took out the next thing, knowing exactly what he was going to say.

He shook his head. "No, Cobey."

"It's my old laptop. Mom and Dad got me a new one when I started college last year. It works just fine," I said. "You might need to clear the hard drive though. It's seen a lot of porn."

His eyes went wide, and he laughed. "Cobey."

I grinned at him. "What? Horny teenager is gonna horny teenager."

At least he was smiling now. "I can't take your things. My old laptop works just fine."

"Vee, it's slower than a stoned sloth." He was about to counter something. "And yours won't last another two years. I've seen how slow it is to run your calc program."

He chewed on the inside of his lip for a bit, staring at the laptop and not looking at me. "I don't know how I feel about this," he said. "I know I don't have new things . . ."

"These aren't new. They're just new*er*. Vincent, they're yours. Do what you want with them. Sell them if you want, give them away. They're yours to do with whatever you want. I just thought you could use them, and honestly, they were just sitting in my room at home." I didn't want him to feel bad. "Or I can take you shopping tomorrow and we can buy you brand-new ones—"

"No!" he barked. Then he laughed incredulously. "God, no."

I sighed. "Are you mad at me? I don't want you to be mad at me. I was just trying to help."

He looked at me then and smiled sadly. "I know, and it's incredibly sweet of you. I've just . . . I've just never been given anything before."

That shocked me. "Never?"

"Not like this. These cost a lot of money. I've never even . . ." He met my eyes and exhaled loudly, his chin a little lower. "I've never even had birthday presents."

He'd never been given anything before, not even for his birthday? Oh my fucking god.

I had to swallow down my rage. And all the hurt and anger, but mostly rage. "You know," I said quietly. "One day I'm gonna meet your dad, and I'm gonna punch him right in the fucking nose."

Vincent smiled, still tinged with sadness. He swallowed hard and looked at the phone and the laptop. "Thank you. For these. I don't know what to say."

"You don't have to say anything." I reached into the bag and pulled out the next thing. It was a neatly folded T-shirt. "Okay, so I asked my mom to grab some of my older stuff because it's smaller." I turned it around and showed him the front. It was just a plain red Tommy Hilfiger T-shirt. Then I pulled out a blue one. "I think I wore them once or twice. They haven't fit me for years, and I'm surprised my mom hasn't cleared them out yet." And then a pair of Nike sweatpants that I last wore in the eighth grade.

I put them in a neat little pile so they weren't so in his face.

"I just thought now you don't have to do laundry so much. Wear them, give them away, or put them in the trash. I don't mind. They're yours."

I reached into the bag and pulled out the phone charger and then the laptop charger, but there was still something else in the bottom. I pulled out a drugstore paper bag with a note taped to the box. "Be safe. Mom," I said, reading it out loud. I knew what was going to be in it before I opened it, and I wasn't surprised at all when I pulled out the box of condoms.

Vincent's eyes went the widest I'd ever seen them. "Oh my god."

Then I pulled out the bottle of lube.

"Oh my god!" He pulled his pillow up to hide his face. "Cobey, make it stop."

I laughed, because at least he wasn't mad about the phone and laptop anymore. I threw the supplies onto my desk, put the folded clothes on his desk, then lay down on my bed. "Can I nap now? I'm tired and my leg's a bit sore." I pulled up the leg of my shorts so he could see the bruise on the outside of my thigh. There were four distinct cleat marks.

Vincent looked, then looked again. "Holy shit. Who did that to you? Is that from yesterday's game?"

I nodded. "Happens a bit. I didn't even feel it in the game. But I bet the guy I smashed hurts more than me today though."

He slid over to sit on the edge of my bed. "If you're hurting, you should have said. What can I do for it?"

I smiled. His concern was so sweet. "You can kiss me. Maybe lie down here with me. Nap for a bit."

I scooted back a little and he folded himself into my arms as the little spoon. As soon as he was settled against me, I sighed and kissed the back of his head and closed my eyes.

"I can't believe your mother sent you condoms and lube," he

mumbled. "For us. She knows we have sex. That means she knew yesterday when she spent the day with me. Oh god."

"She likes you. I knew she would."

He was quiet for a little bit. "I still can't believe she bought sex supplies."

I hummed sleepily. "Well, at least you're not mad at me anymore."

"I'm not mad at you. I'm grateful." He was quick to add, "I'm still teaching you calculus."

# THIRTEEN

## VINCENT

I POINTED TO THE SCREEN. "You're always taking the derivatives when it comes to this guy passing the line of scrimmage."

"He's the running back."

"Right. You make their slope equal to the tangent line. Only this tangent line is the ground."

Cobey stared at the screen, tilted his head. "Huh."

"You see it?"

A slow smile spread across his face. "You know, I think I actually do."

"Good. And now if we look at the definite integral of a player . . ."

Explaining calculus using football was a genius idea. Because he *did* get it. Like Mr. Green had said, on the football field Cobey did the practicality of math every day. Only to Cobey, it wasn't math. It was football.

All I had to do was get him to see the connection, to show him how what he did in a game without even thinking was related to calculus.

And he understood it.

It wasn't easy for him, and I highly doubted he'd ever use calculus again in his life. But he needed to pass this to keep playing football. To stay in school. To stay with me.

All he had to do was get a pass.

I knew he could do it. I had no doubt.

The person I needed to convince was Cobey.

He learned better doing shorter, more frequent lessons. Sitting him down for one long, hard slog meant he'd be zoning out in no time and his brain would put up shutters. So shorter bursts it was.

And it was working.

On the Thursday, one week before his exam, Jayda and I were sitting in the quad waiting for Cobey to come out of his class. His teacher was giving them a study session and time to ask any questions.

We were going through our data structure module, sitting in the sun, minding our own damn business when I heard a guy say, "She's barking up the wrong tree there . . . unless he likes it both ways."

I looked up to see who had said that and who they'd said it to —without thinking it was aimed at us—and of course it was Gavin. He was with two of his friends.

I stared at him, and Jayda put her hand on my arm. "Just ignore him."

"He's a jerk," I mumbled.

Gavin sneered. "What was that?"

"Just leave us alone," Jayda said to him.

"What was that?" He began walking over, and it was clear he'd been waiting to say something to her. His eyes were narrowed on Jayda, his jaw was set. "You wanna speak to me now after you leave me high and dry?"

Jayda closed her book and took my arm, pulling me up and toward the library.

"Yeah, walk away," he called out. "I spent good money on you and got nothing."

I stopped walking.

Because fuck that.

I turned to look at him, scathing at this utter piece of shit. I was so mad I could barely speak. "The fact you think you are owed anything says all there is to know about you. People are not transactional. There is no general ledger in which you are owed anything."

Jayda pulled on my arm again, and I let her drag me away.

"Yeah, you should leave," he called out. "I would say before you do something stupid, but apparently you do him already."

I stopped and turned. It was if the world fell silent. Blood pounded in my ears.

*No one calls Cobey that.*

I saw fucking red. My vision lasered in on him and I had never ever wanted to hit anybody in my entire life, but I closed my fist and zeroed in on him, getting closer with every step.

Until a wall stood in front of me, blocking my path, with the number 33 on his back. Then Nate was there, too. And Cobey was saying something really low and menacing—

"Mr. Green, that's enough," a man barked from the side of the quad. He looked like he could be a young, cool grandpa. If that grandpa was also a drill sergeant.

"Coach," Nate said with a nod.

Shit.

Cobey's coach.

This wasn't good.

We'd amassed quite a crowd.

I couldn't see Gavin, but he mumbled something and Cobey lunged forward and I grabbed his arm, and Nate did too.

"Mr. Stafford," Coach said sharply.

"But—" Gavin tried.

"But nothing. I heard every word you said. Dean's office. Now."

After a tense moment, Gavin turned with a snarl and walked out. Cobey spun around, his eyes wild, his hands quick to cup my arm. "Are you okay?"

I nodded, a little bewildered at the whole ordeal.

"Jayda?" Cobey asked. "You okay?"

She nodded to him, but Cobey slid his hand along my jaw. "Were you going to hit him?"

I nodded. "Right in the fucking mouth."

Cobey snorted and Nate laughed, but Cobey pulled me against him, his heart thrumming against my ear.

Then Coach called out to us. "All of you, this way," he said, holding a room door open.

We filed inside, Jayda, and Nate as well. Coach gestured to some seats. "Please take a seat. I won't be long."

So we sat for what felt like forever.

I really didn't want Cobey to be in trouble with his coach. And then it dawned on me. "Am *I* in trouble?"

Cobey took my hand and threaded our fingers. "Um, I'm not sure yet. Maybe."

I considered this. "I've never been in trouble before."

He sighed. "I'll probably get sidelined. Because it was Coach—"

"That's not fair!"

"Well, you didn't threaten to punch Gavin. I did."

"I was going to."

"I know." Cobey smiled at me. "I heard what he said."

I met his gaze. "No one says that about you. No one."

"Thanks, but if anyone gets expelled or suspended, it'll be me." Cobey shrugged. "I did threaten to beat the fucking shit out of him."

"Expelled?" Fear spiked through me. "What for?"

"I told him if he spoke to you again—"

"But you didn't touch him!"

"Don't think they'll care."

I shook my head. "Absolutely not. I'll tell them it was my fault."

"Vee—"

"Cobey, it'd be the end of your football career. Before it even begins. No way."

"And if you take the rap, you'll lose your scholarship." His eyes were filled with apology and sadness. "No way. If anyone truly deserves to be here, it's you."

I shook my head, really pissed off. "You know what I hate? That assholes like Gavin fucking Stafford get away with everything. They have the connections and the means to simply get away with whatever they want."

"Yeah, I dunno," Nate said. "He's been in trouble before. This won't go over well."

"Gavin's a real jerk," Jayda offered. "I'm sorry for this whole mess."

"It's not your fault," I said adamantly. "What he said was unacceptable. About you, and about Cobey."

Cobey sighed. "I appreciate you sticking up for me," he said, lifting our joined hands and kissing the back of mine. "But you don't have to. I know what people say about me."

"What?"

"What Gavin said. He's not the first."

He'd called him stupid.

Cobey shrugged. "I read the comments on social media. I know they call me a lava lamp."

I squinted. "What does that even mean?"

"Pretty to look at. Not real bright."

I stood up, angrier now than I was at whatshisface. "Cobey, that is not true."

He tried to smile. "Babe—"

"Do not babe me."

"I know what people say about me. That I'm big and stupid. I've heard it my whole life. I can handle it. What I couldn't handle was him thinking he could take it out on you."

"No, fuck him and fuck them." I think he was surprised by my outburst, but god, I was so mad. "All of them. You are *not* stupid,

Cobey. You are not defined by a quiz score or grade or by someone else's opinion."

"There's no point being all mad about it. It's okay, Vee."

Mad? I was past mad. I was livid. "You listen to me. I mean it. Listen to me. Cobey, you are smart. On a football field, who's the one that assesses the plays and who calls the shots? Who does a play-by-play summary of the game and calculates the total yardage for both teams, in his head, while taking down a three-hundred-pound man running full-speed? Who works out numbers, angles, lines, formations, speed, and statistics *while* he's playing? Or on the bench, after he's just run however many miles, making a dozen hits and game calls?"

Cobey gave a shrug.

"You do," I said, pointing my finger at him. "Don't tell me you're stupid. And you don't dare let anyone else tell you that either. You hear me? You think I could do what you do? I couldn't work out any of those equations while making tackles and running like that. Hell, if any of those guys ran at me like they wanted to kill me, I'd crap myself. If I got hit like that, I'd be in traction for a month. And you're out there doing calculus, Cobey, statistics, variables, and percentages on the fly, in your head. Don't you dare let anyone tell you you're stupid."

Nate was smiling and he nudged Cobey. "I like him."

Someone cleared their throat by the door. We all turned to find Dean Kerwin and Coach standing there. The dean was an older woman who totally looked like Jamie Lee Curtis. She wore a skirt-suit and a determined expression, holding some papers in her hand.

Oh no.

"Dean Kerwin," I began. I was still standing, so I squared my shoulders and raised my chin. "I'd just like to say, for the record, blame for the incident should fall on myself, and myself alone. Jayda asked me not to engage with—"

"Please take a seat," she said, walking in and dismissing my attempt to take the blame. I found my seat, and now standing in front of us, she referred to the papers she was holding before looking directly at me. "Mr. Brandt, is it?"

"Yes," I replied. I'd never been in any kind of trouble before and I was strangely calm. "Vincent Brandt."

"Your record is quite impressive," she went on to say. "You're in the top two percent of the student body. Flawless GPA, perfect attendance, in the tutor program. Your high school principal's recommendation was one of the best Franklin U had ever seen, citing your IQ was 140."

Nate leaned forward in his seat so he could gawp at me. Cobey smiled.

I wasn't sure what her point was.

"So," she added, "it would seem today's outburst is out of character for you."

Oh.

"If I may," I said. "I'd like to think today's outburst was an exact measure of my character, not my intelligence."

I think Nate made a choking sound. Cobey took my hand and squeezed it. "Ah, jeez."

I looked at him. "It's true though." Then I looked back at the dean. "I can admit to not thinking rationally, but I cannot apologize for defending the honor and aptitude of my friends. I'll also admit to having limited social parameters, particularly when dealing with targeted harassment and provocation, but I can say, should Gavin Stafford wish to engage in a repeat of his actions, I'll be happy to provide a lesson of correlation versus causation."

Nate stifled a laugh, his shoulders shaking. Coach pressed his lips together so as not to smile. The dean sighed. "There will be no repeat," she said. "I'm issuing an informal caution for you, Mr. Brandt and Mr. Green, and no further action will be taken against you. But—and this goes for all of you—there are avenues for combating harassment. The school will deal with Mr. Stafford, not yourselves."

Cobey and I both nodded.

Then Coach came forward. "I saw the entire incident, and I

heard what was said in the exchange." He turned his focus to Cobey. "You have a responsibility being on my team, son. I won't have misconduct."

"No, Coach."

Then he sighed. "Don't let the likes of Mr. Stafford provoke a reaction from you. You've had a good turn around in your grades this year so far, and you've got a good future ahead of you, Green. Don't let anyone else's behavior take that from you."

"Yes, Coach."

"I don't need to remind you, as a member of the football team, we certainly don't condone threatening violence."

"No, Coach."

"Or—" Coach looked at me. "—providing lessons in correlation versus causation."

I felt thoroughly rebuked, and even though Coach was big and gruff, I liked him. It was easy to see why Cobey respected him.

"Of course, sir."

I was still wondering if I should have called him Coach when we were dismissed, and as soon as Coach and the dean were out of the room, Cobey sighed loudly, but Nate laughed again. "Oh my god, that was too funny."

Cobey turned to him. "Funny?"

"The lesson in correlation and causation," he replied.

Cobey looked at me then. "What was that about anyway?"

"I just offered to help Gavin Stafford reach a scientific conclusion on his actions."

Nate snorted. "A scientific way to say fuck around and find out. That's what he told them," he explained, clapping Cobey on the shoulder. "If Stafford fucks around again, he's gonna find out."

I shrugged one shoulder. "Basically."

Cobey grinned at me, but then his smile turned soft and he took my hand. "You okay?"

I nodded, refusing to acknowledge that I was a little teary.

"You? I'm sorry I yelled at you before. I've never yelled at anyone. I shouldn't have spoken to you like that, and I'm sorry."

He stood up and pulled me to my feet so he could give me a squeezy hug, with his chin resting on top of my head. "It's okay. It was kinda cute." Then he sighed and said, "I want an iced coffee from the coffee shop. Who else is in?"

## COBEY

Having Vincent defend me, getting mad for me, and making a point of telling me how not-stupid I was, was sweet as hell. Sure, his delivery could have used some work, but he was really mad, and these kinds of emotional situations were so new to him.

And he was so cute when he was mad.

*And* he was mad because someone had called me stupid. And then I admitted that other people did too, and he lost his shit. I knew he felt bad about it, but some iced coffee and a few laughs later, he was feeling much better.

Jayda too.

I hated that fuckwit Stafford had said those things about her, but man when he looked about to square up to Vincent was when I lost my shit. I would have flattened him. When he saw me step in front of Vincent, he'd almost shit himself. Went a few shades of gray, for sure.

Not that we had to worry about him anymore.

Franklin U didn't expel him, though there was talk about suspension because he'd been in trouble before, and when his father was called, he had Gavin pack his bags and go back to Utah or wherever the fuck he was from.

I didn't care, as long as he was gone.

Our energy and focus were better spent elsewhere. Vincent really helped me with understanding calc. Once he'd shown me it wasn't some huge impossible foreign language, I wasn't so scared of it.

"It's just the study of continuous change," he'd said. "Did you know the word calculus comes from Latin, meaning small stone? Because we look at all the smaller pieces."

And once I'd learned some terminology and phrases for different equations in simple terms, it wasn't so bad. I mean, it'd have been a whole lot easier if they just called them easier names.

He'd also helped with refreshers for my other classes, which we did in bed, mostly naked.

Studying had never been so much fun.

But a week later I took my calculus final. And I knew without any doubt whatsoever, if it weren't for Vincent, I'd have failed spectacularly.

But I didn't.

He was waiting for me in the quad with Jayda, and he'd been more nervous than me. As I walked out, he stood up, stared at me expectantly . . .

I grinned at him, and he sagged with relief. Then he laughed, then he cried, and he hugged me. "I fucking aced it," I said, lifting him off his feet. Jayda laughed at us.

"I knew you could," he mumbled into my neck.

I put him back on his feet. "You were looking pretty worried there when I came out."

"I knew you could answer the questions but there were unknown variables. Like what if—"

"No more unknown variable shit." I kissed him. "I'm done with that shit forever."

"I'm proud of you."

"Couldn't have done it without you."

"Yes, you would have."

"No, for real. If it weren't for you, the only thing I'd have gotten right on that final was my name."

Vincent sighed happily, then he glanced toward the dining hall. "We were gonna grab coffee."

His frown told me he knew I had training. I kissed the side of his head. "You two have fun. I gotta get to the gym. You've got tutor sessions on this afternoon, right?"

He nodded. "I'll see you for dinner."

I winked at him. "It's a date."

TWO DAYS later the results were in.

I got seventy-four percent.

Seventy-four freaking percent. The highest I'd ever gotten in any math class. Hell, I did better in calculus than I did in marketing. I got seventy-two percent in that one.

Again, way better than I'd have done on my own.

When Vincent came into our room, I was lying on my bed, still on the phone with my parents, telling them the good news. Well, I'd told them about twenty minutes ago . . . they were still yammering on about how proud they were and so happy they'd made the decision for me to move into the dorms. When my mom drew a breath, I took my opportunity. "Okay, I'll text you when I know. Gotta go, love you both. Bye."

Vincent dumped his bag on his desk and eyed me, smiling. "What was that about?"

"Mom and Dad want to take you out for dinner." Then I rolled my eyes. "Well, I assume I'm invited, though I probably should ask them to clarify."

He laughed and came to sit on the edge of my bed. "What for?"

"Because they absolutely know that you're the reason I passed all my classes. And now they love you more than me."

He snorted. "I highly doubt that."

"Well, they're not wrong." He went to say something and I put my hand up. "Nah-uh, none of that 'you just needed to believe in yourself' bullshit. I studied because of you. I tried, and I understood it because of you. I passed because of you."

"I didn't take the finals for you though."

I groaned painfully. "Ugh. Just take the compliment."

He laughed. "Okay, okay. But next semester is biology."

I made a face. "Fucking hell. When does it stop?"

"You will blitz it. You're probably better at it than me."

I rolled my eyes at that. "No more of those unknown variables, right?"

He smiled and shook his head. "None. Not in calc, not with us. No unknown variables."

I rolled my eyes and pulled him down to be the little spoon. "You're such a nerd." I kissed the back of his head. "And Vee?"

"Yeah?"

"Don't ever change."

# EPILOGUE

## VINCENT

"Ugh." I grumbled as I fixed my shirt in the mirror.

A work Christmas party.

Of all the torturous things I had to endure.

Admittedly, I was better at social interactions since college. But this was different.

Data scientist at Apple, if you could believe that. It was entry level but still amazing. I'd been there for ten months. It was great. The people I worked with were great. The money was great. Like *really* great. Not even close to what Cobey was paid, but still more money than I'd ever seen in my life.

And life was great.

Except for Christmas parties and large crowds of people.

I'd graduated top of my class last year and had done some placement work in our final year that looked incredibly good on my résumé. But choosing where I was going to work came down solely to where Cobey was drafted to.

Ultimately, I'd wanted to stay in California but I'd have gone wherever we'd needed to go.

We were a team. We'd been inseparable since our sophomore

year. Never faltered. Not once. We were stronger every year. He was still as sweet and generous as he was back then. Not even pro football could change Cobey Green.

"Come here, babe," Cobey said. He turned me around and proceeded to gently fix a strand of my hair. "Your shirt's fine. You look amazing. Wanna tell me what's really wrong? You haven't been this nervous since the draft."

I cringed inwardly at the memory.

The draft night had been horrendous. I'd been more nervous than he was. He went in with a whatever-will-be-will-be attitude, and I was more of an everything-he's-worked-for-depends-on-this kind of guy. But still, it'd worked out exceptionally well.

He was the second middle linebacker drafted, snagged by the 49ers. And so we moved to San Francisco. Well, more to the point, we moved to Santa Clara. Into a very nice two-bedroom rental, ridiculously overpriced—like holy fucking shit—but it was ours. Well, ours for Cobey's rookie year.

And it suited my career perfectly because hello, Silicon Valley.

For my job that I loved.

Hence the stupid Christmas party.

"I'm nervous because it's the first work-related social event. It's a big deal, everyone will be there, and . . ."

"And?"

"And it'll be the first time being gay in front of them."

Cobey snorted. "Babe, you're gay in front of them every day."

"Yes. But not in front of them, with you."

"Oh. They do know about me, right?"

"Yes, of course!" I said quickly. "They know I live with my boyfriend, and they know your name is Cobey."

He stared at me. "And that's all they know?"

"They know I'm madly in love and unquestionably happy."

"But they don't know I play football?"

I winced. "I can't come out and say that. Not without sounding like a pompous tool. 'Oh hey, yeah, by the way, my boyfriend is *the* Cobey Green, rookie linebacker of the year, totally gorgeous, huuuuuuge dick.' I'm the new guy at work. I barely spoke at all the first month I was there. You know what I'm like around new people. And what if they thought I was name dropping or something?" I shuddered at the thought.

Cobey stared. "So they don't know your Cobey *is me*?"

I pressed my lips together and shook my head.

And he cracked up laughing. "Oh my god. Tonight's gonna be epic. And I'm totally okay with the huge-dick comment, but I can't say your boss would be."

I sighed. "I don't even know if they follow football."

Cobey found that funny too. After he stopped laughing, he looked at himself in the mirror. "Do I look okay?"

I resisted rolling my eyes. "You look like 1.2 million dollars." He looked jaw-droppingly handsome, as per usual. And his ridiculously expensive suit fit him like a well-tailored glove. I'd tried to dress up a little, knowing chances were we'd be photographed tonight, but next to Cobey, I looked like a sack of potatoes.

He grinned. "Come on, let's get this show on the road."

I pocketed my phone and keys. "Oh, Jayda said she can come up for that week you're away next month."

"Awesome. I'm glad you won't be here by yourself."

"And your mom and dad will be here for four days over Christmas."

When we got to the venue, we stopped at the entrance. Well, I stopped and Cobey had to back up a step. Other people arriving were already looking at us. Well, they were looking at Cobey.

"Babe, relax. People love you," he said gently, threading our fingers. "Tonight's gonna be so much fun. And think of it as good practice."

My gaze shot to his. "Practice for what?"

"For my work Christmas party."

"Your what?"

"A Christmas party with the team."

"With . . . with the . . ." My voice squeaked.

He nodded cheerfully.

With an entire NFL football team, apparently.

"I dunno what you're worried about," he said. "I'm about to walk into a room full of geniuses."

I looked at him, staring into those beautiful blue eyes, and smiled. "You know, sometimes I look at my life, at you and at us and at how I got here, and I can't believe all this is real. How lucky I am. And you know what? We've got this, you and me. And we can be surrounded by all the math nerds and all the NFL players, and it doesn't change who we are."

"No unknown variables, right?"

I grinned at him. "Right."

"So are we good?"

I nodded. "Thank you for reminding me."

And with a deep breath, with his hand firmly in mine, we walked inside.


THE END

# MILLSIDE LIBRARY SCORES BIG

SPORTS EDITOR - SAN LUCO TRIBUNAL

**WHEN NFL** star Cobey Green was named Rookie Linebacker of the Year two years ago, he'd had a stellar first season - and he's been racking up impressive stats ever since. But he hasn't let fame or fortune go to his head. One of the highest paid linebackers in the game, Green's latest unbeatable stat is a sizeable donation made to Millside Public Library; a place close to the heart of Cobey Green's partner of six years, Vincent Brandt.

Now a successful data scientist for one of the world's largest tech companies, Brandt spent most of his childhood in the safety of Millside Library. He credits the public library and staff for giving him a place to go for most of his early life. And this year, Green surprised Vincent with a birthday gift he'll never forget. "He doesn't like expensive gifts," Green said. "I didn't know what to get him so I made this donation in his name. He cried when I showed him."

"I couldn't believe it," Brandt said. "It was the most incredible gift. And yes, I cried. The donation will fund a program for underprivileged kids for many years and I can't explain what that means to me."

Green, originally from San Diego, and Brandt, a local from San Luco, met at Franklin University in their sophomore year and they've been inseparable ever since. Green's FU jersey, now signed and framed, hangs in the college bar. "It's been great to come back and visit FU," Green said.

But there's one more stat he'd like to add to his name yet, and it's a personal one. "I asked Vincent to marry me."

And Vincent's answer?

"Yes, of course!" Vincent said with a laugh.

Photo inset: NFL star linebacker, Cobey Green, wearing his famous number 33 for the Franklin U Kings' Championship win three years ago.

# FRANKLIN U BOOKS AND LINKS

## MEET ALL THE COUPLES OF FRANKLIN U!

**Brax and Ty's story:**
Playing Games
**Marshall and Felix's story:**
The Dating Disaster
**Charlie and Liam's story:**
Mr. Romance
**Spencer and Cory's story:**
Bet You
**Chris and Aiden's story:**
The Glow Up
**Cobey and Vincent's story:**
Learning Curve
**Alex and Remy's story:**
Making Waves
**Peyton and Levi's story:**
Football Royalty

Available on Amazon

# ABOUT THE AUTHOR

N.R. Walker is an Australian author, who loves her genre of gay romance. She loves writing and spends far too much time doing it, but wouldn't have it any other way.

She is many things: a mother, a wife, a sister, a writer. She has pretty, pretty boys who live in her head, who don't let her sleep at night unless she gives them life with words.

She likes it when they do dirty, dirty things... but likes it even more when they fall in love.

She used to think having people in her head talking to her was weird, until one day she happened across other writers who told her it was normal.

She's been writing ever since...

# ALSO BY N.R. WALKER

*Lacuna*

*Tic-Tac-Mistletoe*

*Bossy*

*Code Red*

*Dearest Milton James*

*Dearest Malachi Keogh*

*Christmas Wish List*

*Code Blue*

*Davo*

*The Kite*

Printed in the USA
CPSIA information can be obtained
at www.ICGtesting.com
LVHW041544051223
765658LV00005B/534

9 781925 886900